SECRETS!

SECRETS!

Created and written by
LEAH KLEIN

Targum/Feldheim

First published 1993

ISBN 1-56871-036-4

Clipart images from CorelDRAW 4.0 were used in the preparation of this book.

Phototypeset at Targum Press

Printing plates by Frank, Jerusalem

Published by:
Targum Press Inc.
22700 W. Eleven Mile Rd.
Southfield, Mich. 48034

Distributed by:
Feldheim Publishers
200 Airport Executive Park
Spring Valley, N.Y. 10977

Distributed in Israel by:
Targum Press Ltd.
POB 43170
Jerusalem 91430

Printed in Israel

Contents

Contents

1
The *B.Y. Slimes?!*

Nechama Orenstein looked critically at the house in front of her. Taking a deep breath, she yelled, "Hey, Chani! You going to school or what?"

A slight girl with auburn hair and a smattering of freckles across her nose leaned out the opened front door of her home. "Nechama, is that you?"

"Sure is!" Nechama grinned and bounced on her heels. With her short, curly red hair and exuberant personality, sometimes she resembled a comet more than a seventh-grader. "Who else would it be?"

Chani laughed. Who else, indeed? Only Nechama would stand on the sidewalk and yell instead of knocking sedately on the door. "Well, yes, I am going to school or what. Hold on a second and I'll join you." She disappeared back into the house.

Nechama waited patiently for her friend — or as

patiently as she could manage. She whistled quietly to herself, swinging her bookbag. With Purim just a week and a half away, spring was definitely coming to Bloomfield. The breeze was warm and damp, and tiny green buds were beginning to sprout on the trees. Nechama sighed. Who wanted to spend a nice day like this cooped up in school?

After a few moments, Chani reappeared, zipping her lightweight jacket with one hand and juggling her books with the other. She came down the walk to join Nechama, and the two girls strolled down the street together, chatting amiably.

"Where're the Chinns and Batya? They usually walk together with us." Chani looked around, as if expecting her friends to jump out from behind the trees.

"Usually, yeah. But Batya's got a doctor's appointment this morning — she'll be a little late. Chinky had something to take care of — council stuff, I think — and Pinky went with her."

"Uh huh," Chani nodded. The Chinn twins did almost everything together, although in their personalities they were perfect opposites.

"No bookbag?" Nechama asked, hefting her own heavy bag as they waited by the light to cross the street.

"Nope. We didn't get too much homework yesterday."

"You're lucky," Nechama sighed. "We got *tons* of homework. Ten pages of history, three pages of math..." She gave a mock scowl. "How come we poor seventh-graders are getting all this work and you eighth-graders are getting off nice and easy?"

"That's the way it goes," Chani said, matching Nechama's scowl with mock sympathy. "Would it make you feel better if I had a lot of homework, too?"

"Not really, I guess." Nechama grinned again. "I just would rather not have the homework at all!"

"What else is new?" laughed Chani. Nechama wasn't exactly known as a diligent student; fun to be with, sure; the best athlete and *machanayim* player in school, absolutely; a great friend, no question. But studious? Definitely not!

"But I'm glad that we're not getting too much homework now," Chani continued more seriously. "You just watch — right after Purim, every single teacher is suddenly going to realize that she just *has* to give a test before Pesach vacation. And our mothers are going to need us at home to help Pesach clean at the same time. So if we want to get any work done on the Nissan issue of the paper, we're going to have to do it now." Chani, who was editor-in-chief of the school newspaper, put forth a great deal of effort to make sure everything went smoothly with each monthly issue of the *B.Y. Times*.

Nechama whistled. "Boy, Chani, you work fast, don't you? Last month's issue just came out four days ago!" She couldn't help blushing. "No thanks to me, of course."

Chani stopped walking and poked Nechama in the

back. "Hey. Stop blaming yourself. It's over and done with!"

"Yeah..." Nechama grinned sheepishly. "Sorry."

"Don't apologize, either." Chani started walking again. "We had enough apologies last month. I don't want to get into *that* again."

Nechama nodded. Chani was right; the memories of the Adar issue were far from pleasant. Nechama, the distribution manager for the paper, had been piqued by her fellow staff members' apparent lack of appreciation for her hard work. In an effort to make them see how much they needed her, she had gone on strike and pushed her assistant distributor, Ilana Silver, into going along with her. When the strike ploy failed, Nechama had stolen all the copies of the *B.Y. Times* and hidden them away. Afterwards, they'd all apologized to each other: Nechama for hiding the paper, the others for ignoring Nechama and driving her to strike in the first place.

"It was a good issue, though," Nechama remarked. "Pinky did really well on the graphics — "

"That's her job," Chani reminded her, smiling.

"Yeah, I know. And Jen's article on the Festival was also pretty good — "

"That's also her job. She's assistant editor, remember? She's *supposed* to write articles."

" — and the Purim Fun Page was pretty neat, too. As a matter of fact, the whole paper was fantastic —" Nechama grinned. "Or, as Ilana would say, it was 'all right!' "

"Glad to hear you liked it," drawled Chani. "But don't you think you're just a little bit prejudiced?"

"Well, of course I am. But so what? You ask any other kid in Bais Yaakov, and she'll tell you the same thing — the paper is great!"

It was true. The whole student body looked forward to each new issue of the *B.Y. Times*. It was hard to remember a time when the paper hadn't existed.

"And I'll tell you something," Nechama said slowly. "I'm glad I know that everyone likes the *B.Y. Times* so much. If the fourth grade teacher hadn't said anything, I don't think I would have given back the paper."

"What do you mean?"

Nechama looked a little uncomfortable. "Well...last week. You know, when I hid the paper?"

"Yeah," Chani said dryly. "I know."

"Yeah, well, anyway, I was just walking around, you know, and I saw the fourth-graders going into gym class, and they were all excited about Rosh Chodesh coming. I couldn't figure that one out, but then I met their teacher, Mrs. Fogel. She came up to me and said something about how much her girls look forward to every Rosh Chodesh, 'cause that's when they get the paper. And it made me think. When I stole the paper, I wasn't striking only against you and Jen and Pinky and Batya. I was hurting the whole school."

"I see." Chani shifted her books from one arm to the other. "Well, you realized it. That's the important thing." She smiled.

"I guess so," giggled Nechama. With a burst of

exuberance, she skipped a few paces ahead. "And I guess you're right about getting started early this month. Do you want to have a staff meeting today?"

Chani shook her head. "Not today. I've got a big test coming up tomorrow. Tomorrow afternoon, maybe." They turned the corner and walked the last twenty feet to the Bais Yaakov building, joining the stream of girls heading towards school.

"Fine with me." A speculative look appeared on Nechama's face. "I wonder — do you think we can print a picture in the paper next issue?"

"What did you have in mind?" Chani asked curiously.

Nechama grinned. "I think we should print a *certain* picture along with the follow-up story on the Purim Festival."

"That was super, wasn't it?" Chani smiled dreamily. "The best Purim party I've ever been to!"

"Yeah, especially *your* costume," Nechama chuckled. Chani had gone dressed up as Nechama, complete with red curly wig and *machanayim* ball. "So think back, Chani. Remember how Temima Leibowitz from the Student Council was snapping pictures of everything? Well, there's one particular picture that I have in mind." She stopped and eyed Chani, waiting for a reaction.

Chani sat down on the ledge next to the school steps and looked up at her distribution editor. "What are you talking about, Nechama?"

"Come on," Nechama goaded her. "Think!"

Chani frowned in thought. Nechama eased herself down on the ledge next to Chani and waited, a big grin on her face.

"The picture of Chinky handing the winning raffle ticket to Mrs. Blumenkopf?"

"Nope."

"The fifth grade winning the *Tanach* treasure hunt?"

"Try again."

"Ilana Silver as a *Yiddishe mamma* at the health booth?"

"That was something, wasn't it?" mused Nechama. "I think a lot of girls finally realized that the stuff in Ilana's parents' health store actually tastes pretty good. But no, I had something else in mind."

"Hmmm..." Chani smiled wickedly. "How about Rebbetzin Falovitz imitating you in the teacher's *Purim shpiel*?"

Nechama shook her head and gave a mock sigh. "Well, I'd like that, sure. But modesty compels me to refuse the honor. Give up?"

"Well..." Chani's eyes suddenly widened and she burst out laughing. "Oh, no! Not — "

"You got it!" Nechama, a big smile on her face, threw her arms out wide. "Right on the first page of the *B.Y. Times* — Chaya Rochel Chinn, our esteemed student council president, getting hit smack in the face with a wet sponge by our very own faculty advisor and English teacher, Mrs. Handler!"

Chani covered her mouth with her hand, trying to

stop laughing. "Poor Chinky! When they sat her down by the 'Get Haman' booth, nobody dreamed Mrs. Handler would try it..."

"Or be such a good shot, either!"

Chani grinned. "It's a good idea, Nechama — although Chinky probably wouldn't think so."

"Let's do it," Nechama persisted. "Chinky can't complain. She won't sue us, either."

"*Sue* us?!"

"As a former member of the *B.Y. Times*, she just has to make some sacrifices for the good of the paper."

"For the *good* of the *paper*?" Chani looked at Nechama with fond exasperation.

"Yeah, why not? It'll make the paper sell. How's this for a caption? 'Chinky Chinn, former business manager of the *B.Y. Times* and current president of the student council, all washed up!' What do you think?"

"Nechama, you're too much. We don't *sell* the paper, remember? We just give it out." Chani giggled. "If we sold the paper, we wouldn't need a business manager to get ads and raise money!"

"You have a point," Nechama said thoughtfully. "I'd hate to see Batya out of a job."

"Besides," added Chani, "I don't think the picture would come out very well in black-and-white."

"You have a point there, too," Nechama agreed. "Especially since our copy machine isn't exactly up-to-date."

Chani rolled her eyes. "That's putting it mildly!"

Nechama habitually spent more time fixing the machine, yelling at it, and giving it a solid kick in the side than actually running papers off.

"Well, we'll come up with something to make the paper special, Chani. We always do."

The two girls sat in silence for a few moments, savoring the sense of peace that enveloped them both. In another two or three minutes, they would have to rush to get to their classrooms on time; but for now, it was comfortable to just sit quietly together. To their left, a steady stream of girls went up the steps and into the building, talking and laughing.

Chani smiled to herself. Yes, Nechama was right; they *did* have a lot to be proud of. Chani felt so fortunate to have such a wonderful group to work with — Jen, her talented, loyal assistant editor; Pinky, her fellow eighth-grader and close friend, who imbued the *B.Y. Times* with her own good taste; Batya Ben-Levi, the newspaper's resident sabra, who always seemed to know what to say to ease an awkward situation — Batya's father's pizza shop was a favorite meeting place for the staff; Ilana, Nechama's assistant, who, with her relaxed manner and good nature, was friends with just about everybody.

And Nechama. Chani eyed her distribution manager. Life would be so very boring without Nechama....

A sudden giggle made Chani turn her head. She couldn't see anybody, but she could hear girls talking. The hedge that bordered the school building jutted out a little past the ledge next to her, blocking the two of them from the view of anyone sitting on the other side. Chani listened idly for a moment, sorting out the voices. Yocheved Schwartz and Elky Nadel. Sixth-graders. Nice kids.

Then she stopped paying attention to the voices and started listening to the words. Her eyes grew wide with shock, and she sat bolt upright.

"What — "

"Shhhhh!" Chani grabbed Nechama's arm. "Listen!"

Nechama listened to the voices on the other side of the hedge, her mouth slowly opening.

"So...what are we calling it?"

"How about the *B.Y. Crimes*?"

"We could call it the *B.Y. Slimes*!" The giggles rang out.

"Or maybe the *B.Y. Dimes*..."

"The *B.Y. Mimes*!"

"What's a mime?"

"Silent clowns, sort of. They act out little skits without saying anything."

"Nah. How about...the *B.Y. Rhymes*?"

"Hey, that's good! Um...the *B.Y. Limes*?"

"Fruits and vegetables? Why?"

"Well, why not? They're a *berachah*, aren't they? That sort of fits in..."

"I think we should use the *B.Y. Slimes*. It's the funniest."

As Chani listened, her initial shock gave way to a blazing fury. Was *this* what the sixth-graders thought of all their hard work? Was *this* why they put out a paper — so a bunch of kids could laugh at it?

Nechama, too, looked furious, her face flushed and her thousands of freckles standing out in bold relief. She stood up, ready to dive around the hedge and confront Elky and Yocheved. Chani managed to grab the edge of her sleeve and yank her back down.

"No," she hissed. The bell rang, almost drowning out Chani's voice. "Come on. It's time for school..."

Nechama slowly nodded. From around the hedge, Elky and Yocheved came scampering past, not even noticing the two grim-faced *B.Y. Times* staffers standing nearby as they hurried up the school steps. Chani and Nechama followed more slowly, their thoughts dark.

Without saying a word, the two girls trudged through the halls to their classrooms, arriving just in time for the second bell.

"See you later," Nechama said glumly. She yanked open her locker and dug wildly through the stacks of notebooks in search of her siddur.

"Yeah," Chani echoed. "See you later." She turned and dragged herself into the eighth grade classroom.

"Hi, Chani!" Pinky waved. The pretty, vivacious girl was already sitting in her desk, waiting for Mrs. Hershler to arrive. There was something about Pinky that told anyone who looked at her that she was an artist and an expert on colors. "Sorry I couldn't walk with you. Isn't it an absolutely gorgeous day?"

"Yeah, sure. A gorgeous day." Chani slumped into

her seat. Had she really been in a good mood when she left her house that morning?

"What's wrong, Chani? What's the matter?"

"Tell you later," Chani mumbled. She didn't want to talk to anybody. She was feeling much too upset; upset, insulted, distressed, humiliated, annoyed...the vocabulary list went on and on.

It may have been a gorgeous day outside, but Chani didn't really care. All her good feelings, all her satisfaction in her job as editor-in-chief, all her anticipation of putting out a new issue of the paper — were gone.

Vanished.

Gone up in smoke...together with the *B.Y. Slimes*.

2
Davey's Secret

Chani shook her head adamantly. "It's just disgusting, that's all," she declared. "Here we work like crazy, and this is how the student body thanks us." She glanced around at the five others walking home with her, a challenging look in her eye. "Well, don't you agree?"

"Not really," Pinky said carefully, trying to help Chani relax. "Don't you think you're going a little overboard? I mean, kids make fun of things sometimes. Don't you think that's all this is?"

"No, I don't," Chani snapped.

Pinky drew back a little, hurt. Ever-tactful Batya put in persuasively, "I think Pinky's right. It's just a couple of sixth-graders making jokes, that's all."

Nechama snapped her fingers. "Hey, you know what this reminds me of?" She looked at Pinky. "Remember what happened last year, when somebody scribbled graffiti on your sign?"

"You're right!" Pinky exclaimed. "We never even found out who did it. The whole thing just blew over." She looked hopefully at Chani, whose stubborn expression didn't soften. "Maybe this will blow over, too."

Batya looked quizzically from Pinky to Nechama. "How come I don't know what you're talking about? I was on the paper last year, and I don't remember anyone writing graffiti on Pinky's signs."

"Yeah," Jen chimed in. "Tell us. What are you talking about?"

Nechama shrugged her shoulders. "You don't remember it because it happened when you were in Israel, Batya. But you know Pinky's old sign on the door, 'The *B.Y. Times*, Staff Only'? Well, somebody crossed out the word 'staff' and wrote in the word 'snobs' instead."

Jen's jaw dropped. "You're kidding!"

"Nope," Pinky chimed in, an earnest look on her face. "It really happened. And as I remember..." she risked another look at Chani. "Shani felt pretty upset at first, but then she sort of forgot about it. It wasn't really such a big deal, after all." Shani Baum had been the editor of the *B.Y. Times* until she graduated at the end of last year.

Chani stopped walking and glared at Pinky. "And are you trying to tell me that I shouldn't be angry now?"

Pinky swallowed. This was so unlike Chani! "Well, sort of."

"Hmph." Chani started walking again. "Well, you're wrong. This isn't our behavior that's being insulted. Nobody's mad at *us*. It's the paper!" She glanced at Jen, whose loyalty to the *B.Y. Times* was unbelievably strong. "What do you think, Jen?"

Jen frowned. "I don't know, Chani. I'd have to find out more about this before I made up my mind. It may have been something totally innocuous, you know?"

"In-knock-*what*?"

Jen grinned. "Innocuous, Nechama. It means innocent."

"So why can't you just say innocent, then?" Nechama grumbled. "And I'm not so sure it's in-knock-you-whatever you call it. I always thought the *B.Y. Times* was such an asset to the school, and the sixth-graders go around calling it the *B.Y. Dimes* and the *B.Y. Rhymes* and every other silly name they can think of."

Chani turned to the *B.Y. Times'* resident sixth-grader, Ilana Silver, who had kept silent during the whole discussion. "How about *you*, Ilana?" she demanded. "Do you also think this is nothing to get excited about? Do you also think I'm silly to be upset over this?"

"No," Ilana said slowly. "I don't blame you for getting upset. It's just that — " She shrugged helplessly. "I know Elky and Yocheved. They're great kids. I just can't picture them being so nasty."

"Well, they were," Chani said curtly. "And I didn't imagine it. Nechama heard it, too."

Nechama nodded her head, a little reluctantly.

"I don't get it," Ilana sighed. "I don't understand it at all. Elky and Yocheved are two of the best kids in my class..."

Her voice trailed off. Nobody seemed to know what to say next, and the six girls walked on in silence.

Pinky roused herself at the corner of Maple Drive. "You're not going home, Jen?" she asked in an effort to change the subject. "You usually say goodbye to us here."

Jen, equally eager to forget about Elky and Yocheved, answered readily. "I'm going to Batya's today. We're doing a homework assignment together." She grinned at Nechama. "We invited Nechama to join us, but she says she has better things to do than work on history questions!"

"Like what?" Pinky teased her redheaded friend.

Nechama snickered. "The world is full of interesting things, Pinky. I'm sure I can come up with something if I try hard enough."

Batya giggled. "That's Nechama, all right!"

"How's Davey doing?" Ilana asked.

"Davey's fine," Batya replied warmly. As always, her eyes lit up at the thought of her "foster brother." As an only child, it had meant so much to Batya when their family had taken in Davey Eitan, a six-year-old boy whose mother needed to stay in the hospital for observation until she gave birth. "He's so relaxed at our house now." She poked Jen. "Remember the first couple of days, when he wouldn't even talk to us?"

Jen smiled back. She had helped Batya break through Davey's stubborn defenses and convince him that the Ben-Levis could be trusted.

"When is his mother due to give birth?" Nechama asked curiously.

"Pretty soon, I think. Any day now, in fact."

"Davey must be really excited about that," Pinky commented.

A puzzled look crossed Batya's face. "Well, actually, he doesn't seem interested in that at all. He's much more occupied with being a six-year-old boy. You know what I mean?"

"You mean playing in the mud and catching frogs?" Ilana said impishly.

Batya giggled. "Well, yes, he's done that a couple of times! And it seems like almost every one of his friends has a birthday now, so he's always running off to parties. And he just learned how to ride a bike a couple of weeks ago. It's all we can do to get him home before dark!"

"What do you mean, he's not interested that his mother's about to give birth?" Chani asked, intrigued despite herself.

Batya shrugged as they turned onto her block. "We take him to visit his mother every week, on Sunday afternoons. That's the best time, because we can go during visiting hours without missing school. Anyway, Davey skipped his last visit to the hospital, because his best friend Chanan's mother invited him to go bumper bowling."

"Bumper bowling?" Jen repeated. "What's that?"

Batya looked at her, astonished. "You've never heard of bumper bowling? Didn't Melissa ever play it as a kid?"

Jen looked at her, confused. "Is that the same as regular bowling? Jack taught both us of how to bowl when we were pretty young."

"Oh, that's why you don't know. If Melissa can do regular bowling, I guess you wouldn't have to take her bumper bowling." Batya went on to explain. "They put this big plastic tube in the gutters. That way, instead of kids getting gutter balls all the time, it bounces back onto the lane."

"Neat," laughed Jen. "No more zero scores, huh?"

"Exactly." Batya stopped. "We're home! See you guys tomorrow. Bye!"

"Bye, Jen. Bye, Batya," the other four called as the two friends walked up the steps to the Ben-Levis front door.

Batya gave a perfunctory knock on the door before pushing it open. "Hi, I'm home," she called as she led Jen into the front hall.

After a moment, Batya frowned. Usually, her mother called a greeting back — from the kitchen, or the back room where she ran a busy *sheitel* business, or wherever else she was in the house. Why didn't she answer her?

"Ima? Are you home?" A ridiculous question, Batya realized even as she said it. Kind of like asking someone if they were asleep and expecting a "yes" answer.

Footsteps sounded in the kitchen. "Your Ima's sleeping."

The two girls turned. A small boy with dark curls and a smile in his liquid brown eyes stood in the kitchen doorway, regarding them.

"Hi, Davey," Batya smiled. Then her smile disappeared as her "almost-brother's" words sank in. "Ima's *sleeping*?"

"Yeah. She told me a few minutes ago that she's gonna take a nap." Davey was quite obviously uninterested in Mrs. Ben-Levi's sleeping habits. He turned to Jen and asked, "How's your brother?"

Jen suppressed a grin. "Jack is just fine, Davey. He was supposed to go flying today, but he canceled it."

"How come?"

"I don't know, he didn't tell me why. Maybe he didn't want to go flying without you."

"Yeah," Davey agreed, pleased at the notion.

Batya shook her head, a worry line creasing her forehead. "I don't get it. My mother *never* takes naps, except for on Shabbos." She made up her mind. "I'm going to go knock on her door and see if she's okay." She mustered a smile for her "foster brother." "Davey, will you give Jen some cake from the fridge?"

"Okay," Davey said agreeably. He liked Jen a lot — mostly because she was Jack the pilot's sister.

As Batya headed down the hall to check up on her mother, Davey led Jen into the kitchen. He directed her to a chair next to the table.

"Sit down," he ordered. "I'll get you cake."

Jen obediently sat. Davey, obviously relishing the role of host, swaggered over to the refrigerator and took out a platter of cake. He placed it carefully on the table in front of Jen and sat down in a chair across from her. Leaning across the table, he helped himself to a piece.

"You have to take a piece," he said firmly. "Batya said."

"Okay," laughed Jen. She took a piece of chocolate cake, made a *berachah*, and took a bite.

"So what's new, Davey?" she asked.

Davey ducked his head. "Oh, nothin' much."

"Nothing interesting? Nothing exciting happening in school?"

"No, but..." he leaned forward, elbows on the table, and lowered his voice. "I've got a secret."

"You do, huh?" Jen grinned. "Well, what is it?"

"Uh uh." Davey sat back and shook his head. "I'm not telling."

"Okay, then, I'll have to guess." Jen pretended to think hard. "Um...you won a million dollars?"

Davey giggled. "Nope."

"You got a new bike? Batya told me that you just learned how to ride."

"I didn't just learn," Davey said indignantly. "I knew how to ride a bike for three whole weeks!"

"Okay, okay, you're a bike-riding expert," Jen laughed. "Is that your secret? You got a new bike?"

"Nope."

"Hmmm...You have a loose tooth?"

"Nope."

"You're the class spelling champion?"

"Nope."

Jen tried a few more guesses, but Davey just smiled and shook his head to each one.

"Okay, Davey," she said finally. "I guess I have to give up. What's the secret?"

Davey pushed his chair away from the table. "Nope," he said firmly. "I'm not telling." He started to leave the kitchen. He paused at the doorway and looked over his shoulder. "Besides," he added, "it's not so important, anyhow."

Jen watched, grinning, as the six-year-old boy left the room. Moments later, Batya came in.

"How's your mother doing?" Jen asked.

Batya looked a little worried. "She's asleep. I didn't want to wake her up. I just hope everything's okay." She glanced at the platter of cake lying on the table. "I see Davey took good care of you."

"He sure did," Jen chuckled. "Hey, did you know that he has a secret?"

"Yeah? What is it?"

"I don't know. He wouldn't tell me."

Batya grinned. "Kids are like that, aren't they? I remember last month he had this big secret he wouldn't tell anybody. It turned out to be that he had a substitute for Morah Rina."

"Some secret!" Jen giggled. "This secret is probably like that, too."

The two girls left the kitchen and headed towards Batya's room to tackle their homework.

"History," Jen grimaced. "Yuk!"

"Double yuk," Batya agreed. "I never understood the point of history. Why should we bother? I mean, they're all dead anyway!"

"Except for Jewish history, right?" Jen frowned. "Didn't we learn — uh — *maaseh avos siman labanim?*"

Batya looked up and smiled gently. "Yes, we did," she said softly. "That was great, Jen."

Jen flushed slightly at the compliment. "Come on, let's get started."

A little unenthusiastically, they plunged into Chicago of the 1920's. They were deep in question number four when Jen cleared her throat.

"You know, Batya," she said with studied casualness, "Davey's not the only one with a secret."

"Oh?" Batya stopped flipping through the pages of her history book and looked up.

"Yeah. Um...I've got a secret, too."

Batya's dark eyes were filled with curiosity. "Do — do you want to tell me about it?"

Jen smiled a little nervously. "Yes — yes, I think I do." She paused. "I've decided...I've decided..."

"Go on," Batya urged. "That is, if you want to."

Jen hesitated. "Well...I've been thinking about this for a long time." She paused again. "You know how Jack helped me and Melissa become religious."

Batya nodded. Jen's big brother, Jack Farber, had

himself become religious through Rebbetzin Falovitz's family. Jen's parents, while they didn't object to their children being Orthodox, were not yet totally observant themselves.

"Davey's still crazy about Jack," Batya remarked, trying to help Jen feel more at ease about whatever she wanted to talk about. "Ever since Jack took him up for a ride in his airplane, Davey hasn't stopped talking about him."

"Yeah, I know," smiled Jen. "It's the first thing he always asks when he sees me — 'How's your brother?' He once told me that he wants to be a pilot when he grows up, just like Jack."

Batya giggled. "My mother once got him to eat his broccoli by telling him that Jack eats *all* his vegetables."

"Well, don't tell Davey that Jack hates spinach!"

Batya was glad to see that Jen seemed more relaxed. "So...what did you want to tell me?"

Jen chewed her lower lip. "It's hard for me to tell you. I guess it's because you've always been religious."

"You don't have to tell me anything you don't want to," Batya assured her.

"But I *do* want to tell you. Really." Jen took a deep breath. "I've decided that, from now on...I'm not going to read non-Jewish books on Shabbos."

Batya sat up. "Hey, good for you!" she exclaimed.

Jen blushed. "Thanks. I've been thinking about it for a long time now. I knew it would be better if I wasn't reading non-Jewish books on Shabbos, but it's hard for a bookworm like me to make that decision. But it's not really such a hard thing to do, is it? There are so many Jewish books out on the market today."

Batya leaned over and hugged her. "I'm so proud of you, Jen! I'll bet that really was a tough decision to make. It shows how far you've come."

Jen smiled, pleased and embarrassed at the same time. "It wasn't an easy decision, but I'm glad I made it."

The two girls chatted for a while longer. Jen was suffused with a glow of satisfaction. Every step forward was so special for her.

"Well," Batya said reluctantly. "I guess we'd better get back to work." She poked her history book disgustedly.

"Yeah," Jen agreed. "Question number four, here we come!"

Once they stopped talking and got down to work, it didn't take them very long to go through all fifteen questions. Finally, with their homework finished and the Prohibition tucked neatly into their notebooks, the two girls curled up on the bed, laughing and talking. It was six thirty before their *shmoozing* was finally complete (or as complete as two twelve-year-olds' talk can ever be). Batya walked Jen down the hall towards the kitchen for a post-homework snack.

They found Davey in the playroom, absorbed in building a magnificent fortress out of lego. There were little soldiers set up along the battlements, and a Fisher-Price king and queen had set up court inside.

"Very nice, Davey," said Jen admiringly.

Davey ducked his head. "Thanks."

The two girls stood there and watched for a little while. "Jen tells me you have a secret," Batya remarked.

"Yeah." Davey didn't look up.

"What is it?"

"I'm not telling."

"Oh, come on, Davey," Jen coaxed. "I'm not going to be able to sleep if you don't tell me your secret!" Her voice grew dramatic. "I'll stay up all night, staring at the ceiling, wondering what your secret is. Come on, tell me!"

"Nope." Davey moved a soldier down to the drawbridge.

"Aw, c'mon, Davey, talk," Batya laughed. "What's the deep, dark secret?"

Davey finally looked up at the two girls standing side by side. "Oh, all right, I'll tell you," he said. "My Ima had a baby boy today."

3
Jack's Secret

Jen hurried home though the darkening evening, her mind whirling with questions. How crazy could a six-year-old get? Why in the world would Davey react so strangely to the birth of a new baby brother?

When Davey had told his secret, Batya had just stood there, her mouth hanging open in shock. Jen had probably looked the same.

"Your mother had a *baby*?" Batya had blurted. "Why didn't you tell us before? That's great!" She finally recovered herself. "Uh, Mazel Tov, Davey!"

Davey had shrugged. "Oh, I dunno. It's really not so important." And with that, he had returned to his lego fortress as if nothing had happened.

"Of *course* it's important!" Jen had exclaimed. "Davey, aren't you excited? You're a big brother now!"

But Davey had just shrugged his shoulders and

started building another tower on his fortress.

Jen would have liked to stay longer and try to help Batya figure out the reason behind Davey's weird reaction, but she'd promised her mother that she would be home by seven o'clock. Though her house was only three short blocks away, she had no choice but to leave, eliciting a promise from Batya that she would call her later and tell her if she'd gotten anything more out of Davey.

As she turned onto her block, Jen put Davey out of her mind. Instead, her thoughts reverted to the decision she'd made and how she'd confided in Batya. Once again, a warm glow suffused her. She remembered how uneasy she'd felt when she first came to Bais Yaakov. It was the warmth and friendship so generously offered by the Bais Yaakov girls that had really won her over. Batya's heartening words were just another example of how her friends were always encouraging her to take the next step.

To Jen's surprise and delight, an old, battered, white Chrysler was parked in the driveway next to her parents' sleek, gray Mercedes. Super! Jack had come to visit! She generally saw her beloved big brother at least once or twice a week, but it was always a treat when he came to the Farbers' home.

Quickening her steps, Jen hurried up the walk and into the house. She was looking forward to telling Jack about her decision not to read non-Jewish books on Shabbos any more. She knew he'd be proud of her!

The house was strangely quiet. Where was everybody? Automatically, Jen made her way to the family room. To her surprise, nobody was there. That was funny. The comfortable family room, with its casual furniture and cheerful decor, was the favorite hangout for the whole family. Mrs. Farber, an avid amateur interior decorator, had done a beautiful job of designing it. If they weren't there, they must be in the kitchen...

But a quick peek through the kitchen door showed that nobody was there, either. Jen frowned. They wouldn't have all gone for a walk at seven o'clock at night — or if they would have, they wouldn't have left the front door unlocked! What was going on?

Then Jen heard a murmur of voices coming from the living room, punctuated by an occasional burst of laughter. The living room! She'd often wondered why they called it the "living room" — after all, they almost never went in there! It was so formal, seemingly without life. They only used that room for official entertaining, like when one of Mr. Farber's business associates came to dinner. Why would everyone be in there?

Jen hurried down the hall and into the living room with its subdued lighting and paintings on the wall. Sure enough, her whole family was seated on the plastic covered, hard-backed armchairs and couches — Jack and Melissa on the couch, Mr. and Mrs. Farber in twin armchairs, all looking happy and excited and full of anticipation. Something was *definitely* going on!

"Hi, Jen!" Melissa sang out, bursting into a fit of giggles.

"Uh, hi, Melissa. Hi, Mom, Dad, Jack..."

Then she spotted her. Sitting in a corner of the room was a strange girl Jen had never seen before. She looked as if she were in her early twenties, with curly blonde hair, dancing blue eyes, and a hint of a dimple in her right cheek. She was wearing a lacy blouse with a delicate embroidered pattern and a skirt with matching lace trim.

"Jen, we'd like you to meet Shira Zweibel," Mr. Farber said, his voice charged with excitement.

Shira smiled a little shyly at Jen, her dimple leaping into life. Jen started to smile back, and then Jack, too ecstatic for sedate introductions, dropped the bombshell. "Jen, Shira's my kallah! We're getting married!"

"WHAT!?" Jen felt as if someone had slapped her in the face.

Melissa, still giggling, jumped off the couch. "Hooray! Jack's a chasan! *O-o-od yisha-ma be'a-a-rei Yehu-u-dah, u-u-u've'chutzos Yerushalayim...*"

Laughing out loud, Jack jumped up and joined Melissa, dancing with her exuberantly and singing loudly.

"Kol sasso-o-o-n vekol simcha-h-h-h! Kol chasa-a-an vekol kalla-h-h-h!"

Even the Farbers hummed along, clapping and smiling happily at their son. But Jen just stared at Shira, absolutely horrified, while Shira silently stared right back.

"Rebbetzin Falovitz made the *shidduch,"* Jack explained once the atmosphere had calmed down a little. He grinned at his kallah. "See, Shira's mother is an old friend of the Rebbetzin's, so she knows her pretty well. And now that I'm an old man of twenty-seven, I figured that it's high time I got married. So I asked Rebbetzin Falovitz if she had any suggestions, and Shira was the first person she thought of...and the rest is history!"

"But...I...you..." Jen spluttered.

Jack, oblivious to Jen's shock and dismay, chattered on. "Now you know why I've been going to New York so much!"

"You're from New York?" Jen asked stupidly, staring at Shira.

"Yes." Shira spoke for the first time. She had a lovely voice, light and musical. The dimple flashed again. "I'm not from Boro Park, though. My parents live in Lawrence — that's one of the 'Five Towns.' "

"And that's why Jack didn't go flying this afternoon!" giggled Melissa. " 'Cause Shira was coming here!" She clapped her hands. "Jack is a chasan! Jack is a chasan! Jack is a chasan!" Her sing-song tone was definitely getting on Jen's nerves.

"Aren't you going to wish me 'Mazel Tov,' Jen?" Jack teased.

"M-mazel Tov," Jen stammered. "But — but — "

Mrs. Farber, beaming from ear to ear, stood up. "We're so delighted, Jack," she declared. "Now, you said that this engagement party..."

"It's called a *vort*, Mom."

"Not a 'vort,' a 'wart'!" Melissa laughed. She waved her hands in the air as she capered about. "We're going to a warty wed-d-d-ding!"

Jack rumpled his baby sister's hair fondly. "Nope, Melissa, no warts! Anyway, Mom, the *vort* will be next week, on Shushan Purim night." He beamed at his kallah.

"Right," Shira smiled back.

Jen staggered over to the couch and collapsed. "But *Jack*!" she wailed.

"What's the problem, Jen?" Jack grinned down at her. "Don't you want to hear about the wedding?"

"The *wedding*?" Jen almost screamed. "You're getting married already?"

"Not yet," Shira assured her quickly, standing up and coming forward. Even if Jack was too high up in the clouds — without an airplane — to realize the extent of Jen's dismay, Shira obviously recognized that Jen was upset. "Not for another three months. We hope to get married *im yirtzeh Hashem* in May."

"So soon?" Jen gasped.

"Not soon enough for me!" Jack winked at Shira again. "We've got a lot to decide, though. The wedding will probably be in New York..."

Jen moaned.

"But the real question is where we're gonna live."

"What do you mean? W-won't you live here?"

"Well, my company's here, of course, but Shira works in New York. I can always move my base if I have to. That might be easier than Shira trying to find a new job. So we might decide to live there..."

"Live in *New York*!" The words came out in a shriek. Jen's mouth and eyes stretched wide. "But Jack, you — you — "

Jack finally seemed to realize that Jen was just a little upset. "What's bothering you, Jen?"

Jen didn't know what to say — or scream, for that matter. What was bothering her? Besides the fact that her beloved big brother had gone behind her back and gotten engaged to a prima-donna New Yorker who was all frilly and feminine and probably extremely boring and was already planning the *vort* and the wedding and was considering moving to *New York,* of all ridiculous things, far away from Bloomfield, and had apparently told everyone else in the family without breathing a word to her — absolutely nothing!

"Why didn't you tell me?" she finally blurted. It was a start, anyway. She looked half-hopefully up at Jack. He would realize, wouldn't he? He would realize how much he'd hurt her feelings by not telling her about this beforehand. Jack always managed to read her mind, always knew just what to say to make her feel better, always came up with just the right joke to ease a situation. Her big brother would come through now...wouldn't he?

But he didn't. He didn't even seem to realize how angry and upset she was. He was just so wrapped up in his own *simchah*. "Sorry, Jen," he chuckled. "Shira was my special secret."

Shira, however, moved over to the couch where

Jen was sitting in a daze and settled down beside her. "It's nothing personal, Jen," she said quietly. "You see, most people don't like to talk about a *shidduch*, just in case it doesn't work out. They consider it an *ayin hara*, or they don't want to mention anything before they know it's serious. Jack just didn't want to say anything until we were sure that we were getting engaged."

Jen glared at her future sister-in-law. Who did she think she was, anyway? Some patronizing, condescending "frummie" who just loved explaining things to a poor, little *baalas teshuvah*? What made her think Jen wanted to hear her oh-so-sweet explanations?

Jen didn't stop to think that she may have been overreacting. She didn't take the time to really think her feelings through. All she knew was that she was good and mad!

As quickly as she could, she escaped the living room. It didn't help that nobody seemed to notice her leave.

Trembling, she hurried up the stairs, hearing the laughter and animated talk still going on behind her. She ran into her bedroom, resisting the impulse to slam the door. Flinging herself onto her bed, she jammed the pillow over her head in an effort to drown out the last faint sounds of the happy conversation floating up the stairs.

How could Jack do this to her?

Hot, salty tears trickled down her face. She could hardly believe that only half an hour ago, she'd hurried towards the house, eager to tell Jack about her new commitment. And now? Now that he was engaged to Shira, he would probably have no time for her. And besides, would it even mean anything to him anymore? Now that he was engaged to a girl who had always been frum, wouldn't her decision not to read non-Jewish books on Shabbos seem stupid and paltry to him?

She couldn't believe it. She *couldn't*!

But she had to.

Jack was engaged. To Shira Zweibel from New York. With a *vort* next week. Getting married in three months, in New York. Possibly — no, he couldn't! — going away to live in New York.

Nothing would ever be the same again.

4
Stormy Weather

Overnight, the weather changed: from the first gentle hints of spring to a howling gale-force wind complete with spatterings of raindrops. The fierce gusts threatened to tear the new leaves off the trees. Batya and Chani, walking to school together, found themselves being blown down the block, the wind pushing them along and urging them to go faster.

"I've never seen it so windy!" Batya exclaimed, trying to keep her skirt from billowing outward.

Chani, her auburn hair whipping in her face, laughed. "I guess it's really spring. What's that weird expression they say? Something about March coming in like a lion and going out like a lamb?"

"Something like that," chuckled Batya. "And this must be the lion! I just hope we have nicer weather when Davey's father gets here."

"When is he coming?" Chani asked, blinking against the stinging dust the wind blew into her face.

"A day or two before the *bris*. He can't take off any earlier than that."

Chani nodded. "Yeah...I remember you told me that Mr. Eitan had to stay behind in Nigeria because if he left his job, the family would lose their medical insurance."

"Right. That's why we took in Davey in the first place. With Mrs. Eitan in the hospital and Mr. Eitan stuck in Nigeria, there was nobody to take care of him!" Batya grinned. "The *bris* will *im yirtzeh Hashem* be right here in good old Bloomfield. My mother said it looks like they'll be able to have the *bris* on time, too. After that, the whole family will go back to Nigeria..." She sighed, all the excitement leaking away. "It's gonna be real hard to say goodbye to Davey...I guess that's the way things go, huh?"

Chani nodded sympathetically. "Davey must be pretty excited about it, though. It'll be nice for him to be back with his family again."

"Well, that's the weirdest part," Batya said, a strange look crossing her face. "You would think Davey would be on top of the world right now. But he doesn't seem interested at all! Ask Jen — she was there. Davey didn't even want to tell me that his mother had a baby! Can you imagine?"

Chani frowned. "That *is* strange...you say Jen was there? That's strange, too. I spoke to Jen last night about the paper, and she didn't say anything about

Davey. In fact, she didn't talk about anything at all. She sounded kind of distracted."

"Really? Hmmm...and there's more about Davey," Batya went on, talking loudly to be heard over the howl of the wind. "When we told him that his father's coming, he just sort of shrugged his shoulders. He doesn't even seem to care! And when we wanted to take him last night to the hospital to visit his mother and his new baby brother, he refused to go!"

"Really?" Chani shook her head. "I wouldn't get too worried about it, Batya. I mean, sibling rivalry is pretty normal. Davey probably feels a little jealous about all the attention the baby is getting. He'll come around soon enough, don't worry."

"Are you sure?" Batya asked, her voice dubious.

"Oh, yes, I'm sure!" Chani gave a rueful grin. "Believe me, Batya, I know all about sibling rivalry! It *definitely* exists!"

"Oh." Batya bit her lip. Over the last few months, with Davey as her "almost-brother," she'd almost managed to forget the constant, aching loneliness of being the only child. And now, Davey was going away. Like it or not, Batya was going to become an only child once more.

She shook herself. She'd known it was only temporary to begin with. She'd been aware that Davey would only be with them for a few months.

But the knowledge didn't make it any easier.

"When will Mrs. Eitan be able to leave the hospital?" Chani asked in an effort to stop Batya from brooding over Davey's imminent departure.

Batya shrugged her shoulders. "Well, they're not really sure. From what I understand, a mother can usually go home a day or two after giving birth. But Mrs. Eitan is a special case to begin with, so I think they'll be keeping her in the hospital for observation a little longer. In fact, I think she may be released from the hospital the same day Mr. Eitan is coming to Bloomfield."

"And she'll be staying at your house till the *bris*?"

"That's the game plan, anyway."

The two girls reached the corner. Several other girls were standing there, chatting as they waited for the light to change. Here at the corner, with no shield from houses on any side, the wind seemed even wilder than before, whipping skirts furiously and blowing carefully-styled hair into total disarray.

"Hi, Chani!" called one girl, waving cheerfully.

"Hi, Batya!" called another.

"Hey, Batya, I hear you get a Mazel Tov! That's great!"

"Sarah Bayla, I like your headband! Make sure it doesn't blow off."

"Are you ready for that big test today?"

"Did you do that history homework?"

The two girls exchanged friendly greetings with the others as they stood near the curb, waiting for the light to change. Then, just as the light flickered green and the first group of girls stepped into the street, a particularly strong gust of wind came roaring down the street, bending tree branches sideways. The wind snatched at papers and notebooks and sent them flying every which way down the street and into the gutter.

"Agggh! My history homework!"

"Help! Those are my notes for the science test!"

"Somebody catch them, quick! They're gonna get all wet!"

With shrieks of dismay and laughter, the girls went chasing after their runaway papers. Sarah Bayla Eisenman managed to snag several notebooks, while Batya pounced on a few stray homework sheets sailing merrily down the street. Shoshanah Moskowitz managed to rescue Batya's looseleaf. Chani grabbed a pile of papers from the street before they could be run over by the passing cars.

All thoughts of crossing the street were forgotten as the students gathered around to claim their papers. Chani, grinning broadly, read off the name on the top of each page she held and returned them all to their owners.

"See, this is why you always have to write your name on top of every page! Let's see...Estie, this is yours...Batya, here you go...Devorah, here...Elky..."

Chani stopped short, and the smile vanished from her face. Her lips set into a thin, narrow line. "Elky," she said, her voice cold. "Here."

Elky Nadel, an innocent smile on her face, stretched out her hand. "Thanks, Chani," she said brightly. "I'd hate to have to lose that!"

Chani resisted the impulse to scrunch the paper into a ball and hurl it at Elky's face. She handed it over and deliberately turned her back on the sixth-grader.

"What's wrong, Chani?" Batya asked her softly. "What —"

Chani shook her head furiously. Batya could barely hear her voice over the howling wind.

"Emergency meeting today," she hissed, spacing out each word from between clenched teeth. "After school. Spread the word."

Batya stared at her. "Why? What's wrong?"

Chani got herself under control. "I'll tell you then, okay?" She plunged into the crowd of girls crossing the street, leaving Batya standing open-mouthed behind her.

"Hey, Batya!" Nechama shouted as the dark-haired seventh-grader entered the classroom a few minutes before the bell was scheduled to ring. "Mazel Tov!"

"Thanks, Nechama," Batya smiled. "But you already wished me 'Mazel Tov' last night on the phone, remember?"

"Not for you," Nechama wagged her finger. "What, you think you're the only seventh-grader with something special going on in her life?"

"What? Who? Why? Where?" Batya looked around.

Nechama giggled. "Batya, you're too much! And you forgot 'How,' too!"

"Somebody else's mother had a baby besides Davey's?"

"Nope!"

"Well, who's got a Mazel Tov?" Batya demanded impatiently. "It can't be you. Dena's married already!" She grinned. "Unless, of course, you're telling me that *you're* a kallah, too!"

"Not me!" Nechama sang out. "But someone else is!" She executed a quick dance step and gestured dramatically at Jen, who was sitting quietly in her chair without saying a word. "Jen's brother is a chasan!"

"Really? Oh, wow! Mazel Tov!" Batya rushed over to Jen's desk and hugged her. "That's super! When did it happen?"

"Yesterday," Jen said dully.

Batya drew back, a little surprised. "Yeah? How come you didn't tell me?"

Jen lowered her eyes. "I — I just didn't, that's all."

Batya felt altogether confused. She couldn't help comparing Jen's peculiar reaction to the ecstatic hysteria that Nechama had displayed when *her* sister was engaged.

"What's wrong, Jen?" she asked softly.

Jen looked up, her blue eyes flashing. "Nothing," she snapped. "Everything is just dandy."

"Well, okay, if you say so...." Batya's voice trailed off uncertainly. She moved away from Jen's desk and drew Nechama into the corner of the room.

"Nechama, do you have any idea what's wrong

with Jen?" she whispered.

Nechama shrugged, unperturbed. "Nope. In fact, I didn't even find out about Jack from Jen. Jack davens in the same shul as my father, and he told my father that he's a chasan." She shot a look at Jen, who was still sulking in her chair. "Now that you mention it, she *is* acting kinda strange, isn't she?"

"Kinda," Batya agreed. "I hope everything's okay..." Then she remembered. "Chani says there's an emergency meeting after school today."

"How come?"

Batya shook her head. "I don't know. We were walking to school today, and everybody's papers went flying, and Chani collected them."

"And that's why we're having a meeting today?" Nechama sounded a bit confused.

Batya laughed a little. "I guess I'm not doing a very good job of explaining myself! But when Chani started handing everybody's papers back, all of a sudden she got really upset. I couldn't figure out why. And then she told me that there's an emergency meeting after school."

"Oh. Well, I guess we'll find out why at the meeting." Nechama's voice was drowned out by the shrill jangle of the bell, signaling that class was about to begin.

"I guess so..." Batya followed Nechama across the room to where their desks sat side by side. "Remind me to tell Jen about the meeting at recess."

"Yeah. How about Ilana?"

Batya hurriedly slid into her seat as the teacher walked into the room. "Recess time," she hissed out of the side of her mouth.

"Right," Nechama whispered back. Then she faced forward and sat up straight, radiating innocence, attentiveness, and eagerness to learn.

Batya giggled behind her hand. Seventh-grade life just wouldn't be the same without Nechama.

Batya did eventually manage to track Ilana down at recess and pass on the message. She too was inquisitive about the emergency meeting; and when Batya mentioned Elky Nadel's name, Ilana developed worry lines across her forehead. She didn't say anything, though. She just hoped that her uncomfortable suspicions would prove wrong.

Unfortunately, she was absolutely right.

"You heard me," Chani said coldly. "That's exactly what that paper said."

Too upset to sit down in her customary seat at the head of the table, Chani paced around and around the little newsroom, bumping into chairs and tripping over the cord to Dusty, the *B.Y. Times* computer, as she went. Ordinarily, just being in the cheerful newsroom was enough to relax her. With its tasteful decorations — posters drawn by Pinky on one wall, the first page of each back issue of the *B.Y. Times* on another, the certificate they'd won back in November on a third, and the colorful suggestion box in the corner — it was a convivial and friendly work place, with just the right atmosphere for happy and productive meetings.

But today, Chani wasn't in the mood to relax as she circled the table, covered with its pretty lilac cloth. Pacing wasn't exactly the easiest thing to do in the little newsroom. The large table barely fit into the small room, and there was exactly enough room for six chairs, one for each member of the staff, but Chani still managed to pace.

"This doesn't make sense," Pinky almost wailed. "I can't *believe* it!"

"Well, you're going to have to, because I saw it." Chani prowled restlessly around the room, trailing her hand against the wall. "Elky Nadel had a list of things she needs to get: a design for a logo, an editorial, a typewriter, ideas for features and columns, and some kind of advertisement. Sort of sounds like she's making a newspaper of her own, doesn't it?"

There was a short silence. "I admit that it *sounds* like she's working on a newspaper," Batya said carefully, "but..."

"But nothing," Chani cut her off, eyes blazing. "Evidently, the sixth grade has decided that the *B.Y. Times* isn't good enough for them. They're making a paper of their own!"

"Yeah!" shouted Nechama, bouncing in her chair. She didn't really care all that much, but she loved getting involved in things like this.

"We can't let them get away with this!"

"Yeah!"

"Why do we work so hard, if the paper's just going to be made fun of?"

"Yeah!"

"And if we — Nechama, will you *please* stop that?"

Nechama grinned, unrepentant. "Sorry, Chani. I couldn't resist!"

"Now hold on just a second," Pinky interjected. "I know Elky Nadel. She's Aliza Nadel's little sister."

"So? Just because her older sister is a great kid doesn't mean Elky is, too."

"That's not what I mean, Chani. But Aliza's over our house a lot, especially now that she's taking guitar lessons together with Chinky. So I see Elky sometimes, too. And she really *is* a good kid! I don't believe she'd do something like this!"

Chani stopped her restless wandering and stared at Pinky. "Well, you know something? I've got news for you. *She did.*"

Batya, swallowing, tried to defuse the tension. "There's got to be some kind of explanation, Chani. We just have to figure out what it is." Batya *hated* conflict. And this was so unlike Chani! She didn't usually take such things so seriously.

"What other explanation could there be?" Chani demanded. "We've got Elky Nadel writing her own newspaper and calling it the *B.Y. Slimes* or the *B.Y. Crimes* or whatever other nasty name she eventually came up with. And you think there's some other kind of explanation?"

"There *has* to be," Batya said doggedly. "We just

don't know what it is."

Chani started pacing again. "I don't understand why I'm the only one who's upset about this. Jen, doesn't this bother you?"

"Huh? Yeah, sure," Jen said listlessly.

Chani frowned a little; Jen was usually the first person to defend the *B.Y. Times*, like a lioness defending her cubs from attack. Then, shrugging, she waved Jen's strange reaction away. "Pinky? How about you?"

Pinky chose her words with caution. "Well, I think I'd be upset if I was positive the sixth-graders didn't like the paper. But I just don't think that's true — is it, Ilana?" She turned to the staff's resident sixth-grader.

Ilana, who had been sitting quietly and unhappily throughout the meeting, looked up. "No, it's not," she said softly. Her famous Californian smile was nowhere to be seen. "My class loves the paper. Half of them have dreams of being on the staff next year. Nobody thinks the paper's lousy."

Chani glared at her. "Well, then what explanation can you give me for that paper of Elky's?"

"I don't know," Ilana admitted slowly. "But an explanation has *got* to exist."

Chani dropped down into her chair, scowling. "Well, then, what is it?"

Nobody had an explanation to offer. Jen sulked, Chani looked angry, Pinky and Batya felt troubled, Ilana was worried, and Nechama, being Nechama, wasn't disturbed much. Shani had gone into hysterics last year, too, when the word "snobs" was written on Pinky's sign, and in the end it had turned out to be nothing. Why make such a big deal out of this?

Batya finally spoke up. "Before we make up our minds that Elky and her friends hate the paper, I still think we should try to find out what's going on."

Chani sat up. "Yes! That's it!"

"What's it?" Nechama asked, looking around.

Chani pointed a finger at Ilana. "Ilana! You're in the sixth grade."

"Yes," Ilana admitted cautiously.

"So you can have plenty of opportunities to find out what Elky is *really* up to."

"What do you mean?" Ilana asked, beginning to feel a little queasy.

Chani leaned back and folded her arms. "Pretend you're interested in what they're doing. Act friendly. And find out what's going on."

Ilana turned pale. "Y-you mean...spy on my friends."

Chani looked grim. "Exactly."

"I can't do that!" Ilana protested, feeling horrified. "No way!"

"Yes way." Chani stared at her assistant distribution editor. "Ilana, this — is — an — *order*."

Ilana gulped. "But Chani..."

"No buts." Chani glared at the blond sixth-grader. "You are hereby ordered to find out exactly what Elky Nadel is up to. No matter what it takes."

Ilana slumped back in her chair. "Yes, master," she

mumbled as the bell rang, signaling the end of lunch.

Chani pulled herself out of her chair. "I guess we'd better go." She sighed. "We'll meet back here tomorrow to hear what Ilana's found out for us."

Over the years, *B.Y. Times* staff meetings had ended in many different and admittedly unique ways. There was the time when they'd made a *bas mitzvah* party with health food from Ilana's parents' health food store; the time when, split apart by arguments over whether or not to earn money for a trip, they'd marched out on each other; the time when they'd all charged out of the newsroom to find out what was bothering Pinky; the time when Chinky had come bursting into the room to tell them about Mimie Gold in Switzerland. Of course, there were also all the times — in fact, most of the time — when a meeting had ended with chatting and laughter and good feelings all around.

But this was the first and only time that a *B.Y. Times* meeting had ended with the staff members shuffling quietly out without saying a word to each other, each one wrapped up in her own private depressing thoughts.

5
Ilana the Spy!

Ilana walked to school very slowly the following morning. She hated the thought of what she was going to have to do. Wasn't there some way she could get out of it? If only there was no school today, so she wouldn't have to go through with this!

She wished the weather would suddenly drop about forty degrees, so the steady, dreary drizzle could turn into a blizzard and make them close school. Or, if not that, maybe the rain could increase to a real downpour and flood Bais Yaakov. There wouldn't be any school that way, either.

Maybe the boiler could break again. It had only broken twice so far this year, and her classmates had assured her that it usually averaged four or five times during the winter. The only problem with that was that unless the temperature *did* drop forty degrees, it wouldn't be cold enough to close school, anyway.

Failing that, maybe she could suddenly come down with an attack of influenza. Or chicken pox. Or measles. Or appendicitis. Even that would be less uncomfortable than spying on her friends.

Ilana looked hopefully up at the sky, praying for a fresh torrent of rain. As if to spite her, the drizzle thinned out to a barely discernable mist. The sun peeked curiously out from behind the breaking clouds.

Ilana scowled at the sky. "Who asked for good weather?" she demanded aloud.

Maybe she should invest in a disguise. Dark glasses and a stick-on moustache — and a trenchcoat, of course. No spy would be complete without a trench-coat. She hunched her shoulders, her eyes darting right and left as she tiptoed around a tree. There. Now she felt more like a spy. Oh, boy.

As she neared the school building, Ilana indulged in further fantasies. Maybe the teachers were on strike. Maybe the *students* were on strike — although the *B.Y. Times* had certainly had enough of *that* last month. Maybe color war could break out this morning. Or maybe elections...nah, that was always at the end of the year. Maybe she'd be called out of class for some reason. Or how about...

"Hey, Ilana, wake up!"

"Huh?"

Esther Sori Surkin giggled and poked her fellow classmate in the arm. "What are you dreaming about? You almost walked straight into the fire hydrant!"

"I did?" Ilana blinked. "Oh, yeah. I did."

"Come on, class is starting in a minute." Esther Sori tugged Ilana up the school steps.

"Hip, hip, hooray," Ilana muttered under her breath. "Like, I just can't wait."

"What'd you say?"

"Nothing, Esther Sori. Nothing." Ilana followed her friend down the hall and into the sixth grade classroom. Maybe Elky and Yocheved would be absent today. Maybe there would be some kind of assembly. Maybe —

"Sit down, please, girls." Mrs. Eisenstein stood at the front of the room. "It's time to daven."

Obediently, Ilana pulled out her siddur. She had twenty-five minutes left before class would start and she would somehow have to sneak up on her fellow classmates and find out what they're doing.

It was awfully hard for Ilana to concentrate on her davening that morning. Why did she have to spy on Elky and Yocheved, who were both good friends of hers, just because Chani thought they didn't like the paper? But she couldn't *not* do it, either. She valued her friends on the *B.Y. Times* so much. Whether she liked it or not, she couldn't let them down.

How could she make Chani angry by not obeying her orders?

How could she make Elky and Yocheved angry by spying on them?

How did I get myself into this mess???

"Ilana!"

Ilana jumped. "Yes, Mrs. Eisenstein?"

"Aren't you with us this morning?"

"Oh, yes. Yes. Of course." Ilana hastily pulled her *Chumash* out of her desk and opened it up to the right place.

Satisfied, Mrs. Eisenstein began the lesson. But Ilana's mind started wandering again. How would she be able to find out what Elky and Yocheved were doing? Yocheved sat near her — one row over, one seat forward. But Elky was on the other side of the room. She certainly wouldn't be able to spy on *her* in class!

But Yocheved, on the other hand...

Yocheved didn't look like she was paying all that much attention to Mrs. Eisenstein, either. In fact, she kept trading significant glances with Elky, excitement sparkling in her eyes. She constantly flipped the pages of her notebook, taking notes on the morning's lesson on one page and then turning to the back and scribbling something else. Maybe she was working on something for this mysterious substitute paper?

Ilana craned her neck. It wasn't *Chumash* notes, that was for sure. If only she could get a better look...

She cast a quick glance at her teacher. Mrs. Eisenstein had her back to the class, writing something on the board.

Ilana hitched herself forward a little. Now was her chance to get a good look at what Yocheved was doing. Her fellow classmate's notebook was open to that mysterious page. Ilana couldn't make out any words, but she could see lots of scribbles and crossouts. And was that a doodle in the corner? Maybe of a newspaper logo?

Unconsciously, Ilana leaned forward and a little to the right, straining for a better look at Yocheved's notebook. She leaned out a little further, squinting hard. And then a little more. And then a little —

"Whoops!"

Thump.

Crash!

Ilana felt a little disoriented. It's only natural to feel that way when you fall out of your seat and bring your desk down on top of you.

"Ilana, are you okay?"

"What happened?"

"Quick, get that desk off her!"

"I'm all right," Ilana gasped. "I'm all right." With several eager helping hands, she managed to get both herself and her desk upright again.

"Ilana, can you please explain how you managed that?" Mrs. Eisenstein didn't look exactly pleased.

"I don't know, Mrs. Eisenstein," Ilana gulped. "I — I guess I just lost my balance."

"You lost your balance. I see. Well, Ilana, I think I'd appreciate it if you saved your exercises for after class, okay?" Mrs. Eisenstein's voice was crisp but not unkind.

"Yes," Ilana mumbled. "I'm sorry." Smiling weakly at her teacher, she kissed her *Chumash*, which had participated in her tumble to the floor, and reopened it.

Class resumed, more or less. Ilana glared at the back of Yocheved's head. This was all Yocheved's fault, she decided somewhat irrationally. Why couldn't she make it easier for Ilana to spy on her?

Some people just weren't very considerate of others.

Ilana made sure to stay in her seat for the rest of the morning. She didn't need a repeat performance! Besides, she decided, it was silly of her to try to find out what Elky and Yocheved were doing in the middle of class. They'd probably work on their mysterious newspaper during recess. That would be her best chance to find out what was going on.

When the recess bell rang, Ilana eased herself somewhat carefully out of her seat and leaned as casually as she could against the back wall of the classroom, waiting to see what Elky and Yocheved would do. If they put their heads together over Yocheved's notebook, Ilana could artfully drift over there, as if she just wanted to get something out of her desk, and try to see what they were doing. She'd purposely left her snack — carob-coated rice cakes — out on her desk, so she would have a ready excuse.

She could feel her heartbeat accelerating as she waited for the two girls to make their move. Elky was digging into her bookbag — presumably for her own snack — while Yocheved was flipping through her suspect notebook, humming to herself. Ilana pushed a stray wisp of hair that had escaped her ponytail out of her face and waited.

"Hey, Yocheved!" Elky chirped. "Wanna go for a drink?"

Yocheved looked up from the notebook and flipped it shut. "Sure, Elky, sounds like a good idea. Let's go."

Ilana counted silently to ten before following them. She didn't want to stay too close, or they might suspect her.

Fortunately, the hallway outside the sixth grade classroom was pretty crowded with other students going about their recess business. Ilana ducked and weaved her way among the milling girls, feeling her cheeks flush at all the curious glances being sent her way. She knew she looked ridiculous, but she could hardly explain what she was doing.

Sure enough, Elky and Yocheved were standing next to the drinking fountain, chatting and giggling. The mysterious notebook was still closed, but Yocheved kept glancing down at it. They *must* be talking about the newspaper! How could Ilana get close enough to hear?

Maybe if she pretended to be *very* thirsty, and took a long, long, drink of water...

Ilana, straining to look innocent, sauntered up to the fountain. She threw all her effort into not looking at her two fellow classmates, leaning against the wall and talking quietly together. Holding back her long blond ponytail with one hand, Ilana leaned over the water fountain, pushed the button, made a *berachah* and drank.

And drank.

And drank.

As she gulped down yet another mouthful of

water, she strained her ears to hear Elky's and Yocheved's conversation.

"...never realized how hard it was..."

"I guess you have to give them a lot of credit, huh?"

"I'll say! But we have to work on this really hard if we want it come out looking good."

"At least now we have a typewriter. That'll make things easier."

A *typewriter*? Ilana, who was feeling waterlogged by now, listened even harder.

"A computer would've been nice, but — hey, there's Tzivia! Tzivia, wait up!"

Ilana, startled, looked up to see where her quarry was disappearing to. But she forgot that she was still holding the button to the water fountain...

"Hey!" Ilana coughed and spluttered as the spray of water hit her face and soaked her bangs.

"Ilana, are you okay?" Estie Borenstein grabbed her arm and spun her away from the water fountain. "What's wrong with you today? First you fall out of your desk, now this!"

Ilana wiped water off her face. "Thanks, Estie," she gasped. "I'm fine, really..." She caught a glimpse of Elky and Yocheved disappearing into the gym. "Listen, I'll talk to you later, okay?" And with that, she was off and running, chasing after her elusive prey.

Estie stared after her, bemused. There was no question about it. Ilana was *really* acting weird today.

The gym was the most crowded room in Bais

Yaakov of Bloomfield during recess, on days when it was too cold or too wet to play outside. Girls jumping rope, playing *machanayim*, trying to toss a basketball through the hoops, playing tag, or just running or strolling or walking around. All talking and laughing at the top of their lungs. It was practically *impossible* to find one specific person in all that bedlam!

And yet, that was exactly what Ilana had to do. Where were Elky and Yocheved?

The dress code didn't help, either. If she could only be on the lookout for a particular skirt or sweater...but every single girl in the huge gym was wearing the same exact color skirt and blouse: blue. Only shoes and hair styles were different. How would she possibly find them?

Ilana desperately scanned the crowd. There, was that Elky? No, that was another girl with perfectly straight brown hair. Over there? No. Was that her? No...

There! On the other side of the gym! Elky and Yocheved were standing together, poring over the mysterious notebook.

Taking a deep breath, Ilana plunged into the crowd of girls, never taking her eyes off Elky and Yocheved. She just couldn't afford to lose sight of them again. In fact, she was concentrating so hard on her two classmates that she didn't notice where she was going...

"Look out!"

A hand shoved her to one side. Ilana staggered

back as a ball sailed past her nose. Nechama Orenstein leapt out of nowhere to snag the ball and hurl it back at the opposing team.

"Ilana, don't just stand there!"

"Hey, move!"

Ilana looked about her helplessly. Without meaning to, she had wandered right into the middle of the *machanayim* game!

Spinning around, she saw that the ball was heading straight for her. Without thinking, she dodged to the right, slamming into another girl. With a sort of domino effect, six girls ended up on the floor, with Ilana sprawled on top.

"Time out!!!"

Pandemonium reigned in the gym as the six girls struggled to get to their feet. The game came to a ragged halt, with some of the players unaware of what was happening and impatient over the delay.

"Come on, let's get going!"

"Nu? Recess will be over in a second!"

"What's going on over there?"

"Throw the ball already!"

"Me! Me! Throw the ball to me!"

Blushing furiously, Ilana finally managed to stand up, stammering her apologies. She backed away from the crowd, bumping into other players as she went, until she finally reached the relative safety of the back wall.

Panting, Ilana tried to catch her breath, thinking back on the crazy events of the morning. Enough was enough. No more spying for her! She was going to do this the *right* way. The *honest* way.

She waited until her pulse was somewhere down in the lower hundreds. Then, pushing herself away from the wall, she marched right over to Elky and Yocheved.

"Hi, Elky. Hi, Yocheved."

The two girls looked up, Yocheved instinctively slamming the notebook shut. "Hi, Ilana!" Elky said cheerfully. "How ya doing? You must have been pretty bored in class this morning to fall out of your chair." She grinned.

Ilana didn't grin back. "Elky," she said bluntly, "are you making a newspaper to replace the *B.Y. Times*?"

Elky's smile faded, and Yocheved gasped.

"What makes you think so?" Elky asked carefully.

"Just answer the question, okay?"

Elky's smile slowly stole back onto her face. "Do you really want to know what we're doing, Ilana?"

"But, Elky..." Yocheved started to protest.

"Yes," Ilana interrupted. "I do."

"Okay, then. C'mon back to the room, where it's quieter, and we'll show you."

The second the end-of-school bell rang, Chani bolted out of her chair. She didn't even wait for Pinky to join her before dashing down to the newsroom. She yanked the shoestring with the key off her neck and quickly unlocked the door. She flipped on the lights and dropped into her seat, fingers drumming impatiently as she waited for the rest of her staff to arrive.

Jen came into the newsroom a few moments later, together with Batya and Nechama. Pinky was right behind them.

"Sit down, everybody," Chani said tensely. "Ilana's not here yet..."

As if on cue, Ilana came in. "Hi, everyone," she said a little nervously.

"Well? Report!" Chani demanded without giving Ilana a chance to sit down. "Did you find out what Elky Nadel is doing or not?"

Ilana deliberately sat down before replying. "Yes, as a matter of fact, I did. And you can relax, Chani. There's nothing to worry about."

"I'll be the judge of that, thank you very much. What's going on?"

Ilana swallowed. "I can't tell you."

"Whaddaya mean, you can't tell us?" Nechama burst out.

"I can't tell you," Ilana repeated. "Elky showed me what she was doing, but she made me promise not to tell anyone." She took a deep breath. "Chani, can't you trust me? I promise you that Elky's not doing anything to hurt us. It'll be okay."

Chani stared at Ilana, her eyes like granite. Then she looked away. "I suppose I *will* have to trust you," she said stiffly. With a deliberate effort, she pulled herself together. "All right, people. Let's get to work."

The girls shifted in their chairs. Nobody knew

where to look — not at Ilana, not at Chani.

"Okay," Chani said, flipping open her notebook and sighing heavily. "We need a theme."

Pinky's face brightened. *"Simchos!"* she exclaimed. "There are so many *simchos* going on right now — Davey's mother had a baby, and Jen's brother is a chasan. And even if it's Sukkos that's *zman simchaseinu* and not Pesach, getting redeemed from Egypt is a pretty happy thing!" She peered at Chani. "What do you say?"

Actually, Chani said nothing. Neither did Jen, who was still depressed, Batya, who looked troubled, or Ilana, who was obviously uncomfortable with Chani's reaction.

Nechama looked around the silent newsroom. "You know something?" She shook her head at Pinky. "Something tells me that "*simchos*" doesn't quite fit the mood, after all."

6
Shira's Secret

C'mon, Jen!" Jack urged as he hurried out the front door of the Farber's home. "We have to be in Lawrence at 10:30 to pick up Shira, and it's a good hour-and-a-half drive. I don't want to be late!"

Jen followed behind reluctantly. Maybe Melissa was all excited about the idea of spending the day together with Jack and Shira, but Jen could think of a lot more interesting ways of spending her time. Like scrubbing the basement floor, for instance.

Quality time. Jen made a face. That's what they were having now, "quality time." Jack wanted his two sisters to be relaxed and friendly with his future wife, and he figured that a day in New York was just the thing to help them get to know each other better.

The problem was that Jen didn't *want* to know Shira better. And she couldn't understand why

Melissa was so relaxed about all this. Didn't she realize that Jack might be leaving Bloomfield? Didn't she *care*?

Jack was already strapped behind the wheel of his Chrysler, the motor running. Melissa was seated in the back, bouncing up and down excitedly. Automatically, Jen started to get into the front seat next to her brother.

"That's reserved," Melissa called.

"Huh?" Jen stared at her little sister.

"Well, you can sit in the front until we get to Lawrence," Jack offered diplomatically. "After that, you'll have to switch to the back."

So *Shira* could sit in the front. "Of course," Jen said between gritted teeth. "I'll sit in the back, thanks." She flung open the door with a lot more force than necessary and plopped herself down next to Melissa.

Jack frowned for a moment, then shrugged it off. "Okay, folks," he said cheerfully. "We're off!" Whistling, he backed the car out of the driveway, shifted gears, and drove off.

The ride into New York was uneventful, although Jen resisted all of Jack's pleasantries and comments. Melissa, however, more than made up for Jen's sulking with her exuberant excitement.

"What does Shira's house look like?" she demanded.

"It's big, Melissa," Jack replied as he changed to the fast lane of the highway. "About the size of Mom's and Dad's, I'd say. Most of the houses in Lawrence are pretty big."

"I never even heard of Lawrence before," Jen grumbled. And I'd just as soon not be going there, either, she didn't add.

"It's a pretty small Jewish community," Jack explained. "It's probably not much bigger than Bloomfield."

"That's good!" Melissa announced. "That means that Shira's a small-towner. She fits right in with our family!"

"Speak for yourself," Jen growled under her breath.

Finally, they drove off the highway and onto the local streets. Jack slowed down, keeping a wary eye out for street signs.

"Don't you know how to get there?" Melissa asked.

"I sure do, kiddo, but it's pretty easy to get lost here. Let's see...yeah, right, we make a left here. And here we are!" Jack pulled up next to the curb and turned off the engine.

Jen eyed the house suspiciously. It looked nice, with sculpted bushes and an empty flowerbed waiting for summer. But Jen wasn't ready to concede anything. She had a king-sized chip on her shoulder, and nothing was going to relax her.

"Let's go," Jack urged, getting out of the car. Melissa slipped out quickly. Jen moodily opened the car door and stood up, reluctant to enter the Zweibel's house; but Jack was already ringing the doorbell. Pasting an artificial smile on her face, she hurried up the walk to join Jack and Melissa.

Shira herself opened the door, wearing a full, flowered skirt and matching blouse. "Hello!" she said with a warm smile, her dimple flashing in full force. She stood back a little and gestured. "Come on in for a cold drink. Or maybe you'd like something hot?"

"Thanks, Shira," Melissa laughed. "Can I have some Pepsi?"

"You sure can!" Shira showed them into the living room, where her parents — who were much older than Mr. and Mrs. Farber, Jen noticed — were sitting on the couch. "Mom, Dad, I'd like you to meet Jack's sisters. This is Jen, and this is Melissa."

Mr. and Mrs. Zweibel stood up. "Glad to meet you," Mr. Zweibel said gravely.

Mrs. Zweibel, on the other hand, was much more ebullient. "How wonderful!" she bubbled. Jen could see that Shira had inherited her dimple from her. "My, you're a big girl, Melissa. You must be ten or eleven already!"

Melissa beamed, captivated, as Mrs. Zweibel turned to Jen. "And what class are you in, Jen? Eighth? Ninth?"

"Seventh," Jen replied, forcing herself to be polite.

"Come and have a cold drink."

They all sat down at the big table — Jack next to Mr. Zweibel, Shira next to her mother, and Jen and Melissa next to Jack. Melissa eyed the delectable-looking cookies hungrily.

"Help yourself," laughed Shira. "We made them just for you!"

"Don't you have any brothers or sisters?" Melissa asked, looking around.

"I'm the youngest," Shira explained. "Everyone else is married."

"How can you be the youngest? You're much older than me!"

Jen smiled at Melissa's naivete, but Shira didn't. "I'm twenty-three, yes, but I'm still the youngest. *Im yirtzeh Hashem*, when *you're* twenty-three, you'll also still be the youngest."

They spent about twenty minutes chatting amiably before Jack finally glanced at his watch and announced that they'd better get going.

"It was nice meeting you, Mrs. Zweibel," Jen said, almost meaning it. After all, it wasn't Mrs. Zweibel's fault all this was happening. And she was certainly a very nice lady.

"Same here!" Mrs. Zweibel smiled. "I hope we'll be seeing more of you."

Not if I can help it, Jen thought as she followed Jack, Shira, and Melissa out to the car.

Jack drove into downtown Manhattan. With some effort, he managed to find a parking space, and soon the foursome were strolling along, window-shopping.

Jen couldn't help comparing *this* trip with the one she'd taken on Chanukah with all her friends on the *B.Y. Times* staff. They'd also gone window-shopping, but it hadn't been the same. Then, they'd all had the time of their life. Now, Jen was too busy resenting Shira to enjoy herself.

She was glad when they finally got back into the car.

"Well, Shira?" Jack said cheerfully. "We need some directions if we're going to have some lunch!"

Shira smiled. "Where would you girls like to go?" she asked, twisting around to look in the back seat. "There's a pizza shop nearby, and a Chinese restaurant, too. Or if you'd prefer, we can go to a deli. What do you say?"

"The Chinese restaurant!" Melissa shouted. "I wanna eat with chopsticks!"

Shira laughed. "You don't have to eat with chopsticks, Melissa, but I guess you can, if you want to!" She hesitated and looked at Jen. "What about you, Jen? Where do you want to go?"

"I don't really care," Jen said shortly.

Jack frowned and shook his head at Jen, which only made her feel worse. "If Jen doesn't care, let's try out that Chinese restaurant."

"Okay," Shira said, turning round to face front again. "Here, make a right by this traffic light."

"What's your job, Shira?" Melissa asked as they drove to the restaurant.

"I teach special ed," Shira replied.

"You mean, people with learning disabilities, like my friend Sarah?"

"I don't know your friend Sarah," Shira pointed out with a grin. "But have you ever heard of P'tach?"

"Yeah! That's what Sarah does!"

"Okay. Well, the children I work with aren't like

you or Jen. They're kids who have trouble with the ABC's and the *alef beis*, and might not remember today what they learned yesterday. Your goals might be to win a spelling bee or get a hundred on a *Chumash* test, but my students have a long way to go before they can try to win a spelling bee."

Shira paused for a moment. "When I first started, I thought I would want to work with physically-disabled children. I worked with patterning —"

"What's that?" Jen interrupted.

"For kids with very weak muscle control. You move the child's hands or legs through the right pattern over and over again, teaching them how to eat with a spoon, how to walk properly."

"Wow," said Melissa, impressed.

"But I got into special education instead, and — make a left here, Jack. That's right, and into the parking lot."

Jack followed his kallah's instructions and pulled up with a flourish.

"Let's go inside," Melissa said excitedly. "I wanna eat with chopsticks!"

Laughing, Jack, Shira and Melissa got out of the car. Jen got out too, but she wasn't laughing. She followed the other three into the restaurant and settled into a seat at the corner of one of the small tables, making a big show of concentrating on the menu.

When their meal arrived, Melissa was disappointed to see that the restaurant offered regular silverware. "But what about the chopsticks?" she complained.

"Right there, Melissa." Jen pointed to the small, paper-wrapped package lying next to her kid sister's plate.

With a great deal of giggling, Melissa tried to eat with the chopsticks. Shira showed her how.

"How do you know what to do?" Melissa marveled as she finally got the hang of it.

"Shira's talented, that's all," Jack said proudly. He winked at his kallah. "Now, if I can just get her to go flying with me!"

"Haven't you gone yet?" Jen looked surprised.

"We can't go alone," Shira said quickly.

"We'll go along with you," Melissa offered generously.

"Well...we'll see." Shira looked a little uneasy.

Jack chuckled. "Anyone would think you're afraid of flying with me, the way you keep pushing it off!"

"Jack's a good pilot," Melissa assured her earnestly. "You don't have to worry. He won't crash."

Shira smiled weakly, then quickly changed the subject. "Jen, Jack tells me that you work on the school newspaper. What's your job?"

"I'm the assistant editor," Jen said stiffly.

"What do you do? Write articles?"

"Yeah." Jen didn't feel like elaborating.

"How many girls are on the staff?"

"Six." Jen felt resentful. Why did Shira have to pretend to be interested in her?

"What are the other positions?" Shira toyed with her rice.

"Well, Chani Kaufman is editor-in-chief. Pinky is graphics editor..."

"Graphics editor?" Shira put down her chopsticks as her dimple flashed again. "What kind of drawings does she do?"

"Nothing any more, really. We mostly use the graphics from the computer."

"Too bad," Shira laughed.

"Why? What do *you* know about graphics?" Jen challenged.

Shira's eyes twinkled. "Melissa, can I borrow your napkin?"

Curiously, Melissa handed the white napkin over. Shira unfolded it and fished a pen out of her pocketbook. Then, with a mischievous smile, she quickly sketched a caricature of a girl's face with light colored hair held back by a headband, a rounded chin, and large, happy-looking eyes.

Melissa's mouth slowly opened. "*Hey*! That's *me*!"

Shira laughed. "Does that answer your question, Jen?" As she talked, she pulled a second napkin out of the dispenser and started another sketch, this one of Jen. "I've always enjoyed art, and I have this real weakness for drawing cartoons." The caricature of Jen was uncanny. It seemed to capture Jen's gentle sense of humor, her optimistic outlook on life. Jen felt a little uncomfortable as she stared at the sketch. How could Shira see that in her? She certainly hadn't acted like that since they'd met.

"I'd love to get a job as an artist," Shira continued.

"But I love working with special ed, too. So I guess we'll just have to see what happens."

Melissa was tremendously impressed by the two sketches. "There's a publishing company in Bloomfield called 'Sefer Press.' Maybe, if you live in Bloomfield, you can get a job there."

"Maybe," Shira agreed with a smile.

Jen swallowed. It was getting harder and harder to act coldly towards Shira. But she didn't have a choice. She *had* to.

"An aircraft carrier! Wow! It's so big!" Melissa shrieked, trying to look everywhere at once.

Jen leaned over the railing and stared at the Hudson River below. She, too, was fascinated. She'd always liked everything about planes — mostly because of Jack's work as a pilot — and she determined to enjoy herself, even if Shira was along.

"C'mon," Jack called from up ahead. "We can go sit in a fighter jet."

Shira, walking alongside Melissa, stiffened a little. "I'm surprised there aren't more people here," she said. "I expected it to be more crowded."

"Well, we're just lucky, that's all," Jack declared. "This way, if there are only a few tourists around, we can get a better feeling of what it's really like to be in the planes."

"A better feeling," Shira echoed, her face strained. She twisted her hands together.

Stooping to avoid banging their heads in the low

doorway, they entered one of the fighter jets. Sure enough, there were only one or two people there, their noses pressed against the windows looking out.

"The pilot seat is empty!" Melissa crowed. She grabbed Shira's hand and pulled her over. "Here! You be the pilot. Jen and I will be the co-pilots." She pushed Shira into the left-hand seat and sat down in the seat next to her. She grabbed the earphones and put them on her head. Jen, smiling just a little, sat down next to her in the seat furthest right, while Jack wandered through the cockpit, examining everything with professional curiosity.

Melissa reached out and pushed a button. "Control? We're awaiting permission to take off," she said in a deep voice. She turned to Jen. "Roger, we're cleared."

Jen grinned and slipped her own headphones on. "Thank you, Control. We're departing from runway seven at 1400 hours."

The two girls continued talking and pushing buttons. Jen was enjoying herself thoroughly. She almost managed to forget about her future sister-in-law, sitting two seats away. Strange that she wasn't taking part in the fantasy, too...

But Shira wasn't participating in the fun. In fact, Shira's hands were tightly laced together in her lap. Her lips were set in a thin line. And her dimple was nowhere in sight.

Jen watched her, puzzled. What could be wrong?

Then a fragment of conversation floated through

her memory. Jack, talking at lunch: "Now, if I can just get her to go flying with me...Anyone would think you're afraid of flying with me, the way you keep pushing it off..."

Jen stared at Shira. It couldn't be...but it had to be.

Shira was afraid of flying!

Jen quickly turned back to the instrument panel, her mind racing. Jack couldn't know. It must be a secret of Shira's that she was afraid to tell him. And it seemed so surprising — after all, Shira was lively and fun. Jen had heard of people with a fear of flying — Pinky didn't like it very much, either — but she'd never met someone who was so afraid that just sitting in an airplane that wasn't going anywhere gave her the shakes.

"Let's go see the rest of the ship," Shira said brightly as she stood up and made her way back to the entrance. "It must be very interesting."

Jen nodded slowly. Yes. Shira wanted to get off this plane as soon as possible.

The rest of the day passed in a blur. Jen was too preoccupied with her discovery to pay attention to the rest of the trip. Soon, they were standing in the doorway of the Zweibel home, waving good-bye to Shira, as they prepared to start back to Bloomfield.

"Well, guys," Jack said after they were back on the highway. "Did you have a good time?"

"Super!" Melissa enthused. "It was great!"

"How about you, Jen?" Jack looked at her in the

rear-view mirror. "Did you have a good time?"

"Yeah, I guess..." Jen suddenly leaned forward as an idea flashed through her mind. "You know what? How about if the next time Shira comes to Bloomfield, we take her up for a spin in the Cessna?"

"Yeah! Let's!" shouted Melissa, who was always eager to ride in an airplane.

"But Shira keeps pushing it off," Jack frowned.

"So let's not tell her." Jen gave a big, innocent smile. "Let's make it a surprise!"

Jack thought it over, then grinned. "Yeah, that'd be fun. I'll take the two of you with us. We'll have another outing, only this time in the sky!"

"Yeah!" shouted Melissa.

"Yeah," echoed Jen, feeling nastily satisfied. Maybe, when Shira fell apart in the airplane, Jack would see that his wonderful kallah wasn't all that wonderful after all.

A little voice inside wondered if it was a very nice thing to do, but Jen closed her ears to the voice and leaned back against the car seat.

"Yeah," she said again. "It'll be fun. A real, nice surprise...."

7
Abba's Home

Batya slipped the oven mitts over her hands and opened the oven door. A delightful smell wafted through the kitchen as she pulled out a cookie sheet and laid it on the counter. Batya sniffed appreciatively. Chocolate chip cookies — yum!

She smiled happily to herself. There were so many special things happening at once! Just another two days until *Taanis Esther*, and then she had Purim to look forward to, plus Davey's baby brother's *bris* and Jack's *vort*. No question about it — *Mishenichnas Adar, marbin besimchah!*

The first batches of cookies were already cooling on a towel. Brandishing her spatula, Batya started to remove the cookies from the pan and deposit them next to the others. Soon, Davey wandered into the kitchen, attracted by the delicious smell. "Can I have a cookie?" he asked, peering over Batya's shoulder with a hungry look.

"Sure, Davey," smiled Batya. "Here, I'll give you one. Be careful, though. They're still hot." With her spatula, she lifted one cookie up from the baking pan and deposited it on a napkin.

"Thanks," said Davey, clutching the napkin and smiling shyly. "They look good."

"It's all for the *bris* — and *mishloach manos*," Batya laughed. "We have to make sure everything's just right!"

Davey's smile vanished. "Oh," he said. "Maybe I don't want to eat the cookie, after all." He put the napkin back on the counter and started to walk out of the kitchen.

"Hey, Davey! What's wrong?" Batya dropped the spatula onto the counter and hurried after her "almost-brother."

"Nothing. Nothing's wrong." Davey refused to look at her as he scuffed at the kitchen floor with his toe.

"But Davey, aren't you all excited about your Abba coming and — "

"I think I'll go play with my lego fort," Davey announced, pulling away from her. He quickly ran out of the kitchen and into the playroom.

Batya followed after him. "C'mon, Davey. Your Ima's going to come out of the hospital today! Aren't you excited about *that*?"

Davey examined his lego fort carefully. "I've gotta move the king," he said. He picked up the little Fisher-

Price king and moved him to a different room.

"And the baby," Batya persisted doggedly. "Your new baby brother is coming home today, too. Isn't it great?"

Davey frowned at the fort. "I need to make higher walls." Without even looking at Batya, he reached into the lego box, pulled out a handful of blue, yellow and red bricks, and started building.

Batya stared at him, frustrated. "Davey, I'm talking to you, not the wall!"

"Yep. The wall's gotta be higher." Davey carefully built another layer, concentrating on his fort and on absolutely nothing else.

Batya sighed and gave up. It just didn't make any sense...or did it? She sure hoped not....

With a lot less enthusiasm than she'd had a few minutes before, Batya went back to the kitchen and finished taking the cookies off the cookie sheet. She turned off the oven and rinsed off the spatula. Once she'd made sure that the kitchen was as clean as it had been when she'd started, she went to talk to her mother.

Something was bothering Batya. Something she'd kept hidden in the back of her mind, ever since Davey had told her and Jen his "secret." But now, she couldn't stop herself from thinking about it any more. Because if Davey was reacting so strangely to his parents' imminent arrival, could it possibly be that...?

She found her mother sitting in the back room, combing out a thick, blond *sheitel*.

"How is everything, *motek*?" Mrs. Ben-Levi asked with a smile. "Your chocolate chip cookies smell delicious!"

"Thanks, Ima." Batya sat down next to her mother.

"Mr. Eitan will be here soon," Mrs. Ben-Levi remarked. She gave the *sheitel* a critical look. "I just want to get this done first. Mrs. Cohen is coming tonight, and I still have to wash it out..."

"Ima, I — I — "

Mrs. Ben-Levi recognized the signs. Batya wanted to talk. With a faint smile, she put down the *sheitel*. "What's wrong, Batya?"

"It's Davey," Batya confessed, sitting down next to her mother. "I don't understand what's wrong with him! He doesn't want to visit his mother. He doesn't want to see the baby. And he's not even excited that his father's coming in from Nigeria! Every time I try to talk to him about it, he just changes the subject and walks away!"

"He may just be a little jealous of all the attention the baby's getting, *motek*," Mrs. Ben-Levi suggested.

"Well, maybe, but..." Batya hesitated, then finally blurted out her deepest worry. "Ima, what if we did such a good job of taking care of Davey that he wants to stay with us? What if we loved him too much? What if he loves us more than his real parents?"

Mrs. Ben-Levi laughed softly and hugged her only daughter. "There's no such thing as *too much* love, Batyaleh. Everybody has enough love to go around. And while Davey might love us now as much as we love him, he still loves his own family, too." She paused for a moment. "Perhaps Davey is just a little resentful of all the attention the new baby is getting. That's a very natural reaction. Let's just hope he gets over it quickly."

"I hope so," sighed Batya. "I sure hope so."

The sudden chime of the doorbell galvanized Batya into action. "Ima! That must be Mr. Eitan at the door!"

Mrs. Ben-Levi struggled to her feet. "Quick, Batyaleh. Go answer the door. Abba's not here, he's at the pizza shop!"

Batya hurried ahead and ran down the hall. "Davey!" she shouted over her shoulder as she passed by the playroom. "I think it's your Abba!"

But Davey didn't even look up from his fort.

Batya reached the front door and flung it open. She took one look at the man standing on the front porch and gasped.

It was Mr. Eitan, all right. It couldn't be anybody else! And it wasn't the small suitcase he was carrying that gave it away, either. With his curly black hair and beard, his dark complexion, and his deep, liquid brown eyes, Mr. Eitan looked exactly like an older version of Davey.

"Shalom," Mr. Eitan said, smiling tiredly. "You must be Batya." He spoke in a clear Hebrew.

"Shalom, shalom!" Batya stammered. "Please, come in!"

Mrs. Ben-Levi came hurrying to the door, tucking

a few stray hairs into her *tichel*. "*Baruch Haba*, Mr. Eitan! Welcome to our home. Please, come in and sit down."

"Thank you." Mr. Eitan stepped inside and looked around. "Is..." His voice trailed off.

"Batya, call Abba," Mrs. Ben-Levi suggested. "Tell him that Mr. Eitan is here." She smiled apologetically at Davey's father as she closed the door. "My husband is working in our pizza shop. He'll be here soon."

"Thank you," Mr. Eitan said again as he sat down on the couch, putting his suitcase on the floor next to him. He looked around again expectantly, hopefully.

Batya ran into the kitchen and hurriedly dialed the pizza shop, drumming her fingers as she waited for someone to pick up the phone. One ring, two, three...

"Ben-Levi's Pizza Shop," a cheerful voice boomed over the phone. "Can I help you?"

"Abba?" Batya said hurriedly. "Ima says you should come home quick. Davey's father is here!"

"I'm on my way." The phone clicked off.

Batya slammed down the phone herself and bolted out of the kitchen to the living room. She wanted to hear what was happening.

"How was your trip?" Mrs. Ben-Levi was asking as she offered Mr. Eitan a cold drink.

"It was fine," Mr. Eitan replied. "I came here straight from the airport." He looked around again and frowned slightly. "Where — where is Davidi?"

Davidi. Batya rolled the name around her tongue,

liking the way it sounded. Not Davey, *Davidi.*

Mrs. Ben-Levi frowned and jerked her head at Batya. Batya got the hint.

"I'll go get him," she said quickly, jumping up. Mr. Eitan smiled his thanks as Batya hurried out of the room. Where was Davey, anyway? Why wasn't he here in the living room with his father? Why didn't he want to see him?

Batya found him still sitting in the playroom. Davey hadn't moved an inch. He was still absorbed in his fort, building higher walls and moving his soldiers from one spot to another.

"Davey," Batya hissed. "Come into the living room, quick! Your Abba's here!"

Davey looked up and scowled. Batya was taken aback. It was the same expression Davey had worn when he first came to the Ben-Levi house a few months before: sullen and angry, hurt and betrayed.

"Davey!" she gasped. "What is it? What's wrong?"

Davey looked down, but not before Batya glimpsed the tears welling up in his eyes. "Let him go back to the hospital," Davey muttered in a voice almost too low for Batya to hear. "Let him go look at the *baby* again."

"But he hasn't been to the hospital, Davey. He came straight here."

Davey's head slowly came up again. He blinked back the tears swimming in his eyes, and Batya thought she caught of glimmer of something else — could it be hope? "He came straight here?" Davey whispered.

"Yes, Davey." Batya wasn't sure what was happening, but she could tell this was important to her "almost-brother."

"He didn't go to the hospital to see the baby?"

"No, he didn't."

"He came — to me?" Davey swallowed hard.

"Yes, Davey," Batya said quietly, looking him straight in the eye. "He came to you."

Davey slowly put down the soldier he was clutching tightly in his right fist. He stood up and licked his lips. Then, suddenly, without any warning, he raced past Batya towards the living room.

Batya, blinking back tears of her own, ran after him. She got to the living room door in time to see Mr. Eitan stand up, letting his hat tumble to the floor. Davey, his face alight with joy, tumbled into his father's arms.

Mr. Eitan fell back onto the couch from the force of Davey's charge. He hugged his eldest son tightly, tears streaming unashamedly down his cheeks.

"My Davidi," he murmured again and again. "My Davidi."

They sat around the living room table — Mr. Ben-Levi, Mr. Eitan and Davey. Davey refused to sit on a chair of his own. Instead, he shared a chair with his father, clutching him tightly.

"...that would probably be the best way," Mr. Eitan agreed. "I understand that my wife is still not feeling so well. It would be best to make the trip as easy as possible."

"That won't be a problem," Mr. Ben-Levi assured him. "I'll drive you over to the hospital in the station wagon. We can arrange the back seat to be very comfortable for her."

Davey clutched his father's hand even more tightly. "I'm coming too," he announced.

"Of course, Davidi," Mr. Eitan smiled. "You're coming too."

Batya turned away from the door, sniffling. She walked down the hall and into the kitchen.

"It's so *nice*, Ima," she said tearfully. "I'm so happy for Davey!"

"Me, too," Mrs. Ben-Levi said softly. "And I think we can understand Davey's behavior now, can't we?"

Batya nodded, looking thoughtful. "I guess so...He must have thought the only reason why his father was coming to America was for the baby and not for him. No wonder he was angry!"

"But when Mr. Eitan came to the house first, Davey realized that his father loves him, too." Mrs. Ben-Levi opened the refrigerator door and took out a pitcher of orange juice. "You know, Batyaleh, I don't think a six-year-old really understands anything about medical insurance. I'm sure Davey's mother and father explained that Mr. Eitan couldn't leave his job, but I doubt he *understood* it. All he understood was that his father was staying behind...and he thought that meant that his father didn't love him. Now he knows differently."

"Baruch Hashem," Batya sighed. *"Baruch Hashem!"*

She took the pitcher of juice from her mother and carried it into the living room, where the two fathers were still busy discussing logistics. She placed the pitcher on the table next to the platter of cookies.

"I'll be back in a minute with some glasses," she said, winking at Davey. But as she turned to leave, Mr. Eitan held up his hand. "Thank you, Batya, but we really don't have time for juice," he said apologetically. "Davidi and I are eager to go and see the newest little Eitan." He ruffled his son's hair fondly. "Right, Davidi?"

Davey snuggled closer to his father. "Right, Abba," he whispered.

"In that case, we may as well get going," Mr. Ben-Levi said heartily. "Batyaleh, tell your mother that I'm driving the Eitans over to the hospital."

"Can Mrs. Eitan come home now?" she asked. "Will you bring her back here together with the baby?"

Mr. Eitan smiled. "We'll find out," he said. He turned to Batya's father. "Can we call your wife and let her know from the hospital?"

"We certainly can!" Mr. Ben-Levi pushed back his chair and stood up. "Come, Davey. Let's go in the car and pay a visit to your Ima."

"And to my brother," Davey said firmly. "I want to visit my new baby brother."

"Yes, Davey," Mr. Ben-Levi said gently. "And to your brother."

8
Elky's Secret

"Come *on*, Pinky! Your hair looks fine!" Chinky tapped her foot impatiently as she stood in the front hall of the Chinn home, ready to fly out the door as soon as Pinky finished brushing her hair for the twentieth time.

"Okay, okay, I'm coming..." Pinky dropped her brush on the bathroom counter, dashed over to the front hall closet, yanked on her jacket so hard that the hanger fell and landed on the floor, and bolted out the door to join her twin.

"Better late than never, huh?" Pinky winked.

"I guess so," smiled Chinky. "But I'd really rather not be late for school, so let's get a move on! Sarah left ten minutes ago!"

The two auburn-haired girls hurried down the block, hoping to make it to school before the bell rang.

"What's going on with the paper?" Chinky asked

curiously as they waited for the traffic light to change. "You told me Chani's upset about this business of the mysterious sixth grade newspaper."

"It's really weird, Chinks." Pinky frowned. "I've never seen Chani acting like this before."

"She'll get over it eventually," Chinky said philosophically. "It's all a matter of time."

The identical twins always savored their walk to school in the mornings. Unlike their nightly talks, when they discussed their dreams and fears and reviewed the events of the day, their morning walks were a time for practical thinking, for figuring out the solutions to any problems they might have.

"Well, I'm not so sure we've got enough time to wait until she gets out of it." Pinky snuggled into her jacket. "It's almost Purim. Then we only have two weeks until Rosh Chodesh. And we've barely started working on the paper yet! How are we ever going to get this month's issue out on time?"

"That's not your worry, Pinks." Chinky grinned. "Remember what you taught me last month? It's silly to think you can take care of everything." She mimicked her sister's voice. "You've gotta delegate responsibility."

Pinky grinned back at Chinky, but then her smile faded. "But Chani's not taking *any* responsibility. She's too busy sulking." She sighed. "I wish Ilana would tell us what's going on. But all she says is that we have nothing to worry about, and we should trust her."

"Well, why not?"

"Oh, *I* trust her — I think," Pinky amended. "The problem is that Chani doesn't. She's going crazy, trying to figure out what Elky and Yocheved are up too. And she's so busy worrying about this mysterious paper that she's forgotten about the *B.Y. Times*!"

"You have a point there. Usually, she asks me for my column in the first week of the month. But she hasn't mentioned anything yet, not even to give me an idea of the theme so I can know what slant to use." As Student Council President, Chinky wrote a column every month for the paper, called *President's Piece*. Last month, she'd written another article, too, besides three million other things...but that was another story.

"Yeah, well, she can't tell you the theme because we don't have one yet. In fact, we don't have anything!"

"Mm hmm." Chinky looked thoughtful. "So what are you going to do about it?"

"Good question." Pinky frowned. "I'm still working on that one."

"Maybe you can help Chani relax," Chinky suggested. "You know, help her see that she's making a major issue out of something that's really pretty minor. Maybe that would help."

"Maybe. But we've been trying to calm Chani down ever since this whole mess started, and nothing seems to help. She's as prickly as a — as a — as a cactus!"

"A cactus?" Chinky giggled. "How about a porcupine?"

Pinky giggled, too. "Or a thornbush!"

"Well, whatever Chani's as prickly as, I'm sure you'll manage to smooth things over with her," Chinky said as they walked up the steps of the Bais Yaakov building."

"Sure," Pinky said. But she didn't look very confident about it.

"I'll take the *Chafetz Chaim Sez*," Nechama offered.

"Fine." Chani marked it in her book, her pen moving much more slowly than usual. "Maybe you could do something on how secrets can be so insulting to people," she added darkly.

Ilana swallowed.

"And the *Tidbits*? Who's taking that?"

"I will," Batya said. She had a dreamy look on her face. Nobody had to ask why, though. She'd already described Mr. Eitan's emotional reunion with his son about twenty times.

"Great," Chani sighed. "Now we need a theme." She looked gloomily around the table, avoiding Ilana's eye. "Any ideas?"

Jen frowned. "We should do something about Pesach, but concentrate on one angle."

"Like what?" Pinky asked.

"That's the question." Jen drummed her fingers on the table. She was feeling a little too preoccupied to concentrate on potential themes for the Nissan issue of the *B.Y. Times*. The impending flight tomorrow morning, and Shira's inevitable reaction, was all she could think of. "What angles *are* there about Pesach, anyway?"

"Freedom sort of comes to mind," Chani said. "But that's no good." She glowered at Ilana, who shifted uncomfortably in her chair.

"Keeping ourselves separate," suggested Batya. "You know, how the Jews kept their names and their style of clothing and their language in Egypt. We can talk about the necessity of keeping ourselves separate and pure." She cast a wink at Jen. "For example, that we don't read non-Jewish books on Shabbos."

Jen squirmed a little. She'd been so proud of that decision, but her intention to humiliate Shira had taken the edge off her content. No matter how Jack might feel about her reading books, she knew he wouldn't approve of her plans to make Shira look bad.

"That's not good either." Chani scribbled something furiously in her notebook, her pen pressing down so hard it nearly ripped through the page.

"*Achdus*!" Pinky exclaimed. She looked meaningfully at Chani and Batya. "Pesach is when we became the Jewish nation."

"I like that," Nechama said, her eyes lighting up.

"Me, too," agreed Batya. She always liked things about Jews being one big family. Especially now, when Davey was leaving.

"No," muttered Chani. "No good."

"Okay, then," snapped Nechama, feeling a little fed up. "*You* come up with something!"

"I'm too busy thinking about *certain* secrets!" Chani snapped back.

Ilana looked from one girl to another. She opened her mouth and closed it. Then, without a word, she jumped up and raced out of the room.

Everyone stared after her.

"Uh oh," Batya said.

"What do we do now?" Pinky asked.

Nechama crossed her arms. "We're not doing anything until I get my assistant back," she declared.

"Maybe I should go and get her," offered Jen, beginning to stand up.

"No," Chani almost shouted. "I don't want secrets in this newsroom!"

Jen thumped back in her chair, looking a little exasperated. "Chani, don't you think you're taking this too hard?"

"Yeah," Pinky chimed in eagerly. "What's the big deal?"

Even Nechama, who had initially enjoyed the ruckus caused by the *B. Y. Slimes*, was getting tired of having a grumpy editor-in-chief. "Who cares if the sixth grade puts out another paper?" she argued. "*We* know the *B.Y. Times* is great. That's all that matters."

Chani was working herself into a fury. Her face flushed, she bounded to her feet and drew herself up to her full height. "Of course I care!" she yelled. "And I don't understand why you don't! Our paper's going up in smoke and — "

She broke off in mid-tirade as the door opened.

Ilana Silver came into the newsroom, tugging a mystified Elky Nadel behind her.

Chani recovered herself with an effort. "What's *she* doing here?" she asked coldly.

Ilana ignored the question. With uncharacteristic firmness, she walked to the head of the table and stood next to Chani's chair, facing the others. "What we have here," she declared, "is a confrontation. Chani, you want to know Elky's secret. Elky doesn't want anyone to know what she's doing." She turned to Elky. "Elky, you may not realize it, but you've really hurt Chani's feelings."

"I did *what*?" Elky stared first at Ilana, then Chani. The stony look on Chani's face definitely confirmed it. "But I didn't mean to insult you, Chani!" She gulped a little. Most sixth-graders felt just a little awed by eighth-graders, and Elky was no exception. "I didn't mean to insult anybody, really!"

"In that case," Chani said, spacing out each word in her effort to keep her anger under control, "would you care to explain why you're putting out a paper of your own? If you don't want to hurt my feelings or anybody else's, why are you tossing out the *B.Y. Times* and making a new newspaper?"

"But — I — you — " Elky stopped and took a deep breath. "I'm not tossing out the *B.Y. Times,*" she said evenly. "I love the newspaper. I wish I could be on the staff." She paused. "And I'm sorry if you thought that's what I was doing. I really am."

"If that's the case," Ilana prodded gently, "then

don't you think you could tell everyone your secret? It would really help." She glanced at Chani, who still refused to meet her gaze. "If everyone knew what you were doing, nobody would have to be upset about this."

"Oh..." Elky sighed. "I really wanted this to be kept a secret, but I guess *achdus* is more important." She tugged at her ponytail. "But will you all promise, *bli neder*, not to tell anyone else? I want it to be a secret from the rest of the school, even if I have to tell it to you."

Batya, Nechama, Pinky, Jen and Chani all nodded, their faces reflecting their curiosity.

"Okay, then." Elky smiled shyly at them all. "We *are* putting out another paper..."

Chani drew herself up again, ready to explode.

"...as a Purim spoof. A one page paper, as Purim *shtick*." Elky shrugged. "I never thought it would bother you."

For a long minute, Jen, Chani, Pinky, Nechama and Batya all stared at Ilana and Elky.

Then it started. Nechama was the first one to giggle. Pinky started chuckling. Batya tried to smother a laugh. And Jen, who saw no need for restraint, plopped down in her chair and roared with laughter.

"I don't believe it!"

"A *Purim* spoof?"

"*That* was your big secret?"

"All that worrying for nothing!"

"That's hysterical!"

"I don't believe it!"

"Oh, brother..."

Ilana and Elky just stood there, silly grins on their faces. Chani, whose face was beet red from embarrassment, rubbed a hand across her eyes.

"I'm sorry," she apologized, feeling sheepish. "I guess I got sort of carried away..."

"You're telling me," Ilana retorted.

"And all this time, it was just Purim *shtick.*" Chani shook her head, a smile sneaking onto her face. "All this time — all this time —"

And then she, too, began to laugh hysterically. "All that fighting for nothing!" she giggled. "I can't believe it!"

Ilana and Elky just exchanged looks and grinned.

It took some time for the girls to unwind and settle down to the rest of their meeting. Elky remained by Chani's invitation, leaning over Ilana's chair with a mischievous grin on her face.

"You can use our computer, if you want," Jen offered. "That'll make your spoof work out even better."

Elky laughed. "Thanks, but I think it would be better if we stuck to the typewritten version. I'll ask Yocheved, though. She might like the idea."

"All right, then," Chani said briskly, back to her calm, regular self. "So far, we only have our regular columns. We have to get this paper put together."

"And for that, we need a theme," Pinky added.

"Secrets?" Nechama suggested with an impish

grin. "When to keep 'em and when not to keep 'em!"

Chani chuckled. "I guess I deserve that...but we decided last month that we're really sticking to *mitzvos bein adam lachaveiro*, didn't we? And I'm not so sure secrets really qualify." Her face suddenly turned thoughtful. "Although in a way, it really does..."

"I have an idea," Batya interrupted. "Pinky said it before. *Achdus*! It's the perfect theme. And we can talk about how keeping secrets can drive friends apart, too."

Jen's face brightened. "Hey, I could write a poem about that!"

"And it would make a great editorial," Chani added.

"And Chinky could write about *achdus* on the Student Council," Pinky added.

"Well?" Chani looked around the staff room, her pen hovering over her notebook. "Are we agreed? Is achdus our theme?"

Pinky nodded. So did Batya, Nechama, and Jen.

And Ilana? She twisted in her chair and winked at Elky.

"You know something, Chani?" she said. "*Achdus* sounds absolutely perfect."

9
Jen's Secret

Jen hummed to herself as she strolled along the few short blocks to Batya's house. In just another hour or two, she, Melissa, Jack and Shira would be on their way to the airport. She was looking forward to going up — she always enjoyed it.

Then her humming stopped. She frowned to herself. *Shira* wouldn't enjoy it...

She shrugged her shoulders. Well, it was going to happen. Jack would've eventually found out how Shira felt about flying, anyway. This way...he would just find out a little bit earlier.

As Jen neared Batya's house, her steps quickened. With the *vort* in three days and Davey's brother's *bris* on the same day, Jen was determined that she and Batya would take care of everything they needed to do for the paper first. That way, they wouldn't let Chani and the others down.

Jen felt very strongly about the paper. She always had, from the first day she'd stepped into the little newsroom, nervous and too frightened to show it. She may have put on a show of arrogance to hide her apprehensions, but she'd loved the *B.Y. Times* from the very beginning.

So today, Jen was going over to Batya's house to make sure that her friend had already gotten her ads together, as well as the *Class Tidbits* she'd volunteered to collect. She herself had just finished polishing her poem on *achdus*. They would be able to hand their work over to Chani and then concentrate on their own respective *simchos* without any guilt feelings.

Or could they? Could Jen really not have any guilt feelings — if not about the paper, then about what she was doing to Shira?

Jen shook her head impatiently. Why was she worrying so much about it? It was going to happen, and that was that!

With a nod, feeling satisfied at squelching any lingering doubts, Jen knocked briskly at the Ben-Levi's door.

"Come on in!" said a muffled voice from inside.

Jen pushed open the door and walked in. "It's Jen Farber," she called.

"Hi, Jen! Come on into the living room," Batya called back.

Jen obediently followed the sound of Batya's voice and found herself in the living room. She'd never seen the room so crowded before! Batya was there, of course, together with her parents. And Davey was there, together with *his* parents. And the baby was there, too!

"Mazel Tov, Mrs. Eitan," Jen said warmly. "I'm Jen Farber."

"Thank you," Mrs. Eitan replied in somewhat halting English.

Davey, curled up on the couch next to his mother, tugged the sleeve of her pretty housecoat. "Ima, Jen is my friend," he said importantly. "And she has a big brother who flies planes! And when I grow up, I'm gonna fly planes, too!"

"Whatever you want, Davidi," Mrs. Eitan smiled.

Batya sat in an armchair, beaming from ear to ear. "Tell Jen what you did before, Davey," she suggested.

Davey gave Jen a brilliant smile. "I held my little brother!" he said proudly. "All by myself!"

"Good for you, Davey," Jen laughed.

Davey turned to his mother. "Ima, can I do it again? Can I? Huh? Please?"

Mrs. Eitan surrendered with a laugh. "Okay, *motek*. Sit back..."

Jen watched, smiling, as Mrs. Eitan ever so gently deposited her newborn son into Davey's arms. Davey's face was all aglow with pride as he cradled his baby brother.

After a few moments, Jen finally remembered why she'd come. "I'm sorry to bother you, Batya, but could you give me your ads and stuff?"

"Huh? Oh, yeah, sure. Come on into my bedroom."

Batya turned to her guests. "I'll be back in a minute," she excused herself. Then she and Jen left the living room.

"How much longer are the Eitans going to be in America?" Jen asked as they strolled down the hall.

Batya sighed. "Three more days after the *bris*. They have to wait that long, so it'll be safe for the baby to travel. After that..." She shrugged. "They're planning to go back to Nigeria for another two months. Then Mr. Eitan's job will be finished, and they can go back to Israel."

"You'll miss Davey, won't you?" Jen asked sympathetically.

"Well, sure, of course I'll miss him." Batya spoke slowly and thoughtfully. "It'll be quiet when he's gone," she sighed. "But that's life, I guess. People move on. And I ought to be glad that he's finally back with his family, where he belongs." She shrugged her shoulders. "I can't hold on to him. It's not supposed to be that way." She paused for a moment, thinking. "I'd love if he could stay here...but this isn't where he's supposed to be. He's supposed to be with his family." She mustered a smile. "It's not as if I'm losing him completely, anyway. We'll still stay in touch. I'll just have to get used to not having him around anymore, that's all."

Batya didn't seem to notice how quiet Jen became as the two girls entered her bedroom. She rummaged through her folder and dug out the advertisements she'd collected and the *Tidbits* she'd gathered in the last few days.

"Here you go, Jen," she said, holding them out.

"Huh? Oh, yeah, thanks. Thanks." Jen absent-mindedly took the papers, her mind obviously somewhere else.

"Jen? Is everything okay?"

"What? Oh, yeah, sure. Um...I'd better get going. I'll see you later, okay? Thanks for the stuff." Jen gave Batya an abstracted smile as she left the room and headed down the hall towards the front door.

A little bemused, Batya followed her guest to the door and watched her set off down the sidewalk. That was weird, she thought. I wonder what that was all about?

Jen walked quickly home, her head bent against the wind, her mind churning. Batya's casual words hammered through her brain again and again.

"...That's life, I guess. People move on...I can't hold on to him. It's not supposed to be that way...It's not as if I'm losing him completely, anyway. We'll still stay in touch. I'll just have to get used to not having him around anymore, that's all...I ought to be glad...I ought to be glad..."

Jen shivered. Batya could have been speaking for her! Wasn't she trying to cling to her brother, when it was really time for him to move on?

"It's not as if I'm losing him completely...I can't hold on to him..."

She *wasn't* losing Jack completely. He was getting married, that's all. Moving on.

"I ought to be glad..."

Shouldn't she be glad for Jack? Shouldn't she be happy for him?

Yes, she should. And — Jen lifted her head, her eyes widening with surprise — she *was*.

Jack was engaged to a wonderful girl, lively and full of fun. And nice. She'd kept trying to befriend Jen, but Jen hadn't let her. Look how much Melissa liked her! It should have been that way with Jen, too...except that Jen was too upset and angry to think straight.

"It's not as if I'm losing him completely, anyway..."

Jen's mouth twisted into a rueful smile. It wasn't too late, was it? She could start again, really get to know Shira better. In fact, she would have the opportunity to start afresh in just half an hour, when they all went to the airport to —

Jen stopped short and turned pale. The airport! They were going up in a plane — and Shira was terrified of flying! Instead of having the chance to tell Jack quietly, Shira would be forced to admit her fears in the most embarrassing and humiliating way possible — and it would all be Jen's fault!

Would could she *do*? Jen's mind raced as she hurried up the walk to her own home. She couldn't tell Jack to cancel the trip — not without revealing Shira's secret. But if she didn't say anything, Shira's secret would come out, anyway!

Unless...

Unless...

A slow smile spread over Jen's face. Yes. That was it.

The perfect solution...

Jen bounced up the steps and into the house. "I'm home, Mom!" she sang out as she raced up the stairs to her room, dumping Batya's papers on her desk. She'd have to hurry and change; Jack would be coming to pick her and Melissa up in just a few minutes. Jack — and Shira.

She just hoped she'd be able to find a minute to talk with Shira someplace where Jack — and Melissa — couldn't hear. Because she and her future sister-in-law had something very personal — and very private — to talk about.

"Right," Jack said cheerfully. He patted the gleaming wing of the Cessna 150/150. "So what do you think, Shira?"

Shira licked dry lips. Her dimple was nowhere in sight. "You keep it looking very polished," she managed.

"Well, of course," Jack chuckled. "Gotta look good for my customers!"

Jen watched her brother and his kallah anxiously. So far, all attempts to get Shira alone had met with failure. Melissa, who was obviously struck with adoration for her future sister-in-law, clung to Shira's side. And Jack, who was bursting with pride, insisted on explaining everything in sight to Shira in complete detail. How would Jen manage to have an urgent, private talk with Shira before they went up?

"So, are you ready?" Jack rubbed his hands together.

Shira swallowed. "I — I g-guess so."

"Good." Jack strode toward the plane. "I can file a flight plan on board, so — "

"Hey," Jen interrupted. "Melissa never saw you file a flight plan before. Why don't you take her over to the control tower?"

"Yeah!" Melissa chimed eagerly. "Can I see the control tower?"

Jack looked from Melissa to Jen to Shira, puzzled. "Well..."

"Go ahead," Jen urged, casually taking Shira's hand. "Shira and I will board and make ourselves comfortable."

"Are you sure?" Jack looked at his kallah inquiringly.

Shira hesitated.

Melissa tugged impatiently at Jack's sleeve. "C'mon, Jack, please? I wanna see the control tower!"

"Okay, okay," Jack laughed, surrendering. "We'll be right back, Shira." Swinging Melissa's hand, he strode off.

The second they were out of sight, Jen turned to Shira.

"Listen," she whispered urgently. "I know some people are scared of flying..."

Shira jumped. "What?"

"You're one of them, aren't you, Shira? You're

scared of flying, right?"

Shira swallowed. "Yes. Y-yes, I am. I get the shakes just thinking about going up in a plane. And I haven't — I didn't tell Jack. I meant to, but — and now — and now — "

Jen squeezed her hand. "It'll be our secret," she told her quietly.

"But — but — "

There was no time to say anything else. Jack and Melissa were already coming back.

"It'll be our secret," Jen repeated in a murmur as Jack came striding up.

"Hey, I thought you two were going to board already!" Jack teased.

Shira opened her mouth, but Jen squeezed her hand again and said loudly, "It'll be great, Shira — you and me together in the back. I'll be with you all the way."

Shira flashed her a startled glance. Jen smiled enigmatically back.

"Let's go," Melissa urged as she climbed aboard the Cessna. "Let's go already!"

The foursome boarded the plane, Jen steering Shira to a seat towards the back.

"Why back there?" Jack frowned at Jen. "Let Shira come sit up here in the front."

"Shira wants to let Melissa sit up front," Jen said quickly. "Right, Shira?"

"Right." Shira managed a faint smile. "I'll have lots of opportunities, Jack. Let Melissa have a chance."

"If you say so..." Jack, still looking a little puzzled, slipped into the pilot's seat and put his headphones on. Melissa, beaming with excitement, sat down next to him. Jen and Shira settled into seats behind them, Shira's hand gripping Jen's like a vise.

Jack turned around and smiled at his kallah. "Ready?"

"Ready," Shira said faintly.

"Great!" Jack turned back to the controls and spoke into his mouthpiece. A few moments later, the plane eased out of the hangar, heading towards the runway.

Shira was trembling, biting down on her lower lip, her face white. Jen, holding her hand, stroked her fingers lightly.

"Relax," she whispered. "It'll be okay."

The plane picked up speed. Jack looked cool and competent, an expert at what he was doing. Melissa, strapped into her seat, managed to bounce up and down anyway.

"We're lifting!" she shrieked. "We're going up!"

Light as thistledown, the Cessna abandoned the ground and rose into the clear blue sky. Shira shut her eyes and swallowed convulsively. Jen murmured soothing words, still holding onto her future sister-in-law's hand.

"We'll be leveling off soon," she assured her in a low voice. "Don't worry." She raised her voice. "Hey, Jack, let's have a smooth ride, okay? I'm not in the mood for acrobatics."

Jack didn't take his eyes off the controls. "Okay by me," he replied absently. "Shira?"

Shira took a deep breath. "I'm not in the mood for acrobatics, either," she quavered. Fortunately, Jack didn't seem to notice how shaky her voice was.

"Okay." The plane leveled off. Jack flew a little longer, then switched onto autopilot. He took off his headphones and turned around. "How are you two doing in the back?"

Just in time, Jen sat up and snatched her hand away from Shira. Shira, startled by Jen's sudden movement, opened her eyes and smiled back at her chasan. "Just fine, Jack."

"Great." Jack leaned back in his chair. "We're on autopilot now. The plane's doing all the flying!"

Shira gulped, and Jen ever-so-casually stretched out her legs. "It's perfectly safe like this, of course," she mused aloud to no one in particular. "They fly like this overseas all the time."

"Really?" Shira asked weakly.

Jen nodded firmly. "Really."

They flew on for another half an hour. Gradually, slowly, Shira began to relax, although she still didn't seem entirely at ease. Every time the plane banked, she would stiffen and grab wildly for Jen's hand, but as she realized that they were still safely in the air, she would sink back into her own seat again.

Then they were heading downwards. All of Shira's fears seemed to return at once. With her blue eyes opened wide and her teeth clenched tightly together,

Shira clung to Jen's hand, while Jen whispered calm assurances.

"We'll be on the ground soon," she murmured over and over. "It's okay."

And it was okay. The plane touched ground smoothly, without the slightest hint of a bump. The engines roared and the Cessna slowed down, coming to the end of the runway and turning back toward the hangar.

Shira's breath was coming in gasps, but she still managed to summon up a smile every time Jack looked back at her.

"Here we are!" Jack brought the Cessna to a stop and switched off the engine. He pulled the headphones off and turned to look at Shira. "So, how was it?"

Safely on the ground, Shira was able to smile more easily. "You're a great pilot," she said warmly. She touched Jen's hand for reassurance. "It was a really smooth ride."

"I should hope so!" Jack unbuckled his seat belt and stood up. "C'mon, guys. Shira and I will take you to Ben-Levi's for pizza!"

"Yay!" cheered Melissa, following Jack out of the plane. Jen and Shira were right behind them.

"I'll go get the car," Jack offered. "You can all wait here." He strode off without waiting for an answer.

Shira and Jen smiled conspiratorially at each other. Melissa bounced over to where Hank, their older cousin who shared the business with Jack, was working on the Piper Cub.

"Thanks, Jen," Shira said gratefully. She ran a hand through her soft blond curls and breathed an exaggerated sigh of relief. "I *never* would have made it without you!" She grinned at Jen, her dimple flashing in full force. "Who knows? Maybe some day I'll even enjoy it!"

The two of them laughed. "Don't worry, Shira," Jen assured her. "I won't tell anyone. It'll be our secret."

Shira's face turned serious. "Really, Jen. I never would have managed if you hadn't helped me."

"That's okay," Jen said. Then, shyly, she added, "...Sis."

10
Batya's Secret

The high, thin wail of the eight-day-old little boy rose above the voice of the *mohel*, then died down to a small whimper as the baby was given a pacifier dipped in wine to suck. Jen moved a corner of the *mechitzah*'s curtain aside and craned her neck, trying to see exactly what was going on in the other room. She'd never been to a *bris* before, and it was all so fascinating! Nechama stood next to her on tip-toes, beaming with excitement.

There was an expectant pause, and then the *mohel* said in a loud, clear voice, *"Yehonatan ben Yosef zeh hakatan gadol yihiyeh."*

Jen, following carefully along in her siddur, recited aloud with the others, *"K'shem shenichnas labris, kach yikaneis l'Torah, l'chupah, u'l'maasim tovim."* The *B.Y. Times*ers exchanged glances and smiles.

The *mohel* recited the *mi shebeirach*. Mr. Eitan's Israeli accent made his voice easy to distinguish as he intoned the *yehi ratzon*.

"Amein, kein yehi ratzon!" everyone declared.

Pinky clapped her hands with excitement, Ilana waved a fist in encouragement, and Chani blinked back tears. She always cried at times like this — *brissim*, weddings, engagement parties — no matter how hard she tried to control herself. Chinky, standing nearby, silently handed her a tissue, then blew her own nose. "Mazel tov!" she whispered.

Batya, her dark eyes shining and her cheeks flushed, beckoned to Jen, who followed her friend out of the *ezras nashim* into the hallway. There, Mrs. Ben-Levi was standing by the door of the men's section, waiting for her husband to bring the baby to her.

Jen looked around curiously. "Where's Mrs. Eitan?" she whispered to Batya. She didn't want Mrs. Ben-Levi to overhear.

Batya grinned. "My mother told me that it's very hard for the mother of the baby to be present at the *bris*. She's waiting in the kiddush room for my mother to bring the baby to her."

"Not *the baby*, Batya. Yehonatan," Jen corrected with a grin of her own.

"Right, Yehonatan." Batya pointed at her mother. Mr. Ben-Levi was just handing his wife the softly-whimpering baby, who was lying on a beautiful white, embroidered pillow. "See? The Eitans gave my parents the honor of *kvater*. That means that my father carries the baby to the *mohel* and then brings him back to my mother. Then my mother will take him to Mrs. Eitan."

Jen nodded, absolutely fascinated. Mrs. Ben-Levi, a tender look on her face, cradled the pillow with little Yehonatan in her arms, crooning softly.

Batya continued her explanation. "Being the *kvater* is considered a *segulah* for having children of your own." She didn't realize her mother overheard the remark, but Mrs. Ben-Levi looked up and suppressed a smile.

"A *segulah*? Like that red thread from Kever Rochel that people wear as a bracelet?"

"Yeah, sort of. There are all sorts of *segulos* for all kinds of things. There's even a place in Eretz Yisrael called *Amukah*, where it's a *segulah* for finding a chasan or kallah if you daven there!" Batya watched her mother walk down the hall with the pillow, heading towards the kiddush room, then turned back to Jen. "Let's go back inside. They're gonna say *aleinu* now, and then we'll go have the *seudah*."

The two girls hurried back inside and finished davening. Then, with their siddurim put away, they joined the stream of ladies walking towards the kiddush room for the *seudah*.

As they entered the kiddush room, Batya continued explaining things to Jen. "It's a mitzvah to attend a *bris*, so you're not supposed to actually *invite* someone. You just call them up and tell them what time the *bris* will be."

Chani, who had offered to make some of the phone calls, overheard and laughed. "After a while, you begin to sound like a tape recording!" She let her eyes glaze over and recited in a monotone, "There will be a *bris im yirtzeh Hashem* tomorrow morning in the Mogen Avrohom shul. Davening is at seven-thirty. The kiddush will be right after davening."

Jen giggled. "You're right. It *does* sound like a tape recording!"

The *B.Y. Times*ers sat together at one table, drinking soda, eating cake, laughing and talking.

"Yehonatan!" Chinky exclaimed as she poured herself a glass of soda. "That's so cute — and so perfect!"

"What do you mean?" Jen asked.

"I get it," Pinky broke in. "David and Yehonatan. You know, King Shaul's son and David Hamelech. They were best friends, ready to sacrifice everything for each other."

"That's right," Chani agreed. "Yehonatan helped David escape from Shaul, even though he knew that if he helped his father capture David, he himself would become king!"

"And now we've got two brothers named David and Yehonatan!" Ilana laughed. "All right!"

Nechama gave a mock sigh. "Do you mean the poor things won't be able to fight with each other?"

Jen kicked her under the table.

"It's sure been an exciting month, hasn't it?" mused Batya. "It started with the Purim Festival on Rosh Chodesh..."

"And then Jack got engaged!" Jen added happily. Happily! *Baruch Hashem*, she was able to feel happy about it. It felt as if a dark cloud had evaporated from her mind. She felt so happy for Jack and Shira now — and so much better herself.

"And Mrs. Eitan had a baby," Pinky continued, going on with the list.

"And we thought we had a rival newspaper," Ilana teased as Chani blushed good-naturedly.

"And yesterday was Purim!" Nechama chimed in, a gleam in her eye.

"And today's Shushan Purim...starting with a *bris* and ending with a *vort*!" Pinky finished with a laugh.

"It's hard to believe Purim's over," Pinky remarked. "But we've got enough nosh left in the house to last until Pesach, that's for sure!"

"What about caramels?" Chinky teased.

Pinky shook her head emphatically. "Nope, not for me! I'm not going to start gaining weight again!"

"Good for you, Pinky!" Chani exclaimed.

"But we still have to get rid of the nosh somehow," Nechama said practically. "And the only way to do *that* is...to eat it!"

They all burst out laughing.

"If I see another hamentash, I'm going to scream," Chinky moaned. "I even dreamed about hamentashen last night!"

"Did you dress up when you went out delivering *mishloach manos*?" Ilana asked Nechama.

"Nah. But I took my nephew around. He was

dressed up like Achashveirosh."

"My, my, how original!"

"Well, what do you expect from a four-year-old?"

Batya felt a pang. She wouldn't know what to expect from a four-year-old. For a little while, she'd had some experience with a six-year-old, but now...

"Who can eat chicken at nine o'clock in the morning?" Pinky grumbled.

"Ah, ah! It's a mitzvah!" Chani chided.

"I know," Pinky sighed, picking up her fork. "A *bris* is a *seudas mitzvah*. But if I eat chicken...I can't eat caramels!"

Chinky giggled. "I thought you weren't eating them anymore!"

"Oh, I'm not. But it would nice to know I could if I wanted to."

Nechama rolled her eyes. "Pinky, that makes as much sense as...as..."

"As my getting hysterical over the *B.Y. Slimes*," Chani finished, winking at Ilana.

The girls quieted down as Mr. Eitan got up to speak. Batya understood most of what he was saying, and most of the others managed to follow along, but Jen and Ilana, whose backgrounds in Ivrit were weak, were completely at a loss. Bored, they concentrated on turning their plastic cups into plastic spiders, tearing strips down the sides and holding them upside down.

All too soon, it was time to say *birkas hamazon*. Nechama looked at her watch hopefully.

"A quarter to ten. There are only two hours left of

school. Do you think our mothers will make us go?"

"I'll bet we're the only Bais Yaakov in the *whole world* with school on Shushan Purim," Pinky complained.

Chinky laughed. "Well, they don't have any school in Yerushalayim, that's for sure!"

Chani's eyes turned dreamy. "Can you imagine having Purim twice in a row? You could do that if you lived in Eretz Yisrael. You know, spend Purim in Bnei Brak or Tzefas or something, and then go up to Yerushalayim for Shushan Purim. You would hear the megillah four times, give *mishloach manos* two days in a row..."

"...And have to eat two *seudos*!" Jen finished with a giggle. "I don't think I could handle that!"

"Well, we'll have to do it today," Chinky reminded everyone with a grin. "We've had this *seudah*, and then we're going to have to eat another *seudah* tonight at Jack and Shira's *vort*!"

"No, you won't," Jen assured them. "We're not having a big meal. Just a sort of open house at the Zweibel's, cake and soda and fruit." She looked anxiously from one girl to another. "You're all coming, aren't you?"

"We wouldn't miss it for anything!" Batya said fervently.

"No way!" Nechama chimed in. "My father said he'll take us all in the station wagon. We daven in the same shul as the Farbers, so my parents are invited, too."

"Good." Jen smiled her relief.

Slowly, reluctantly, the girls stood up.

"I guess we'd better get going," Chani sighed. She looked around. "Can we help clean up, Batya?"

"It's okay," Batya said. "We've got everything under control."

Still, the girls helped put all the leftover cake onto one platter and clear off the disposable tablecloths. As Nechama said, "This way, we've got an excuse not to go to school!"

By eleven o'clock, they were all finished. Waving their good-byes, they left the shul and headed for their respective homes.

Batya watched them go, smiling. If she had to be an only child, she sure had the most phenomenal friends in the world...

"Batya?"

Batya turned her head. Her mother came up to her, a mysterious smile on her lips.

"Hi, Ima. Where's Mrs. Eitan? And Davey? And Yehonatan?"

"Abba drove them home," Mrs. Ben-Levi replied. "The *mohel* went along with them. He's going to show Mrs. Eitan how to bathe Yehonatan over the next few days."

"The next few days..." Batya repeated, her smile fading away. "And then they're leaving." She looked up at her mother. "I'm really going to miss Davey, Ima."

"Yes, I know. So will I." Mrs. Ben-Levi paused.

"But I wanted to tell you about something, *motek*. Something that's going to happen this summer..."

Mrs. Farber smiled at Mrs. Zweibel as the two women grasped the pretty china plate wrapped securely in a cloth napkin. Shira, standing to one side, looked beautiful: she wore a delicate pink silk dress with a faint flora pattern. Her blue eyes were glowing with happiness.

The two mothers banged the plate against the back of a chair. With a muffled *crack*, the plate broke in two.

"Mazel tov!" Everyone chorused.

Jen and her friends stood just outside the doorway, watching excitedly. It was the second *vort* they'd had in just a few months — first Nechama's sister, and now Jen's brother!

"We're becoming real experts!" Ilana laughed.

Jen grinned at Batya. "I hear that it's a *segulah* to collect pieces of the broken plate — the seventh one you collect is supposed to be from your *own vort*!"

Batya smiled, seemingly lit up from the inside, as if an excitement was fizzing just beneath the surface. "*Segulos*," she murmured to nobody in particular.

They made their way back to the room where the women were standing, sitting and talking. Jen marveled at Shira's siblings. She'd known that Shira was the youngest, but she didn't think that Jack was going to have nieces and nephews older than she was! In fact, Shira had a twenty-year-old niece that was already married and expecting a baby. Jack was going to be a great-uncle at the age of twenty-eight!

Shira came floating back into the room, her cheeks flushed. "How are you doing, Jen?" she asked.

Jen winked at her. "Me? I'm *flying high*!"

Shira shared a private smile with her future sister-in-law. "Thanks," she whispered. Then she turned to talk to one of her seminary friends who had come to the *vort*.

Jen wandered across the room to where her friends were standing around. Pinky was busy admiring everyone's outfits. Chinky and Chani were talking animatedly about when the wedding would be, and what *shtick* they could take along to dance with. Ilana and Batya were busy comparing everything to Dena Orenstein's *vort*. And Nechama was eating every piece of seven-layer cake she could get her hands on.

"It's gorgeous," Nechama told Jen though a mouthful of crumbs. "Almost as nice as my sister's *vort* was."

Jen wagged a finger at her. "You're just prejudiced!"

"Well, of *course*!"

Chani glanced anxiously at her watch. "Nechama, you don't think your father's going to want to leave soon, do you?"

Nechama glanced at her own watch and made a face. "Yeah, probably. He's gonna want to be home before midnight, I think, and it'll take over an hour, even at night when there's no traffic. That means we'll have to leave in — " she made a rapid mental calculation " — fifteen minutes."

"Too bad," Ilana said philosophically. "That's the way it goes."

"And then we are going to *buckle down* and get to work," Chani said firmly. "Rosh Chodesh is only two weeks away. We've got most of our articles written up, but we still have to get them typed into the computer. And Pinky has to set the paper up, and then we'll have to print it out and run it off and collate and — "

"Hey, hey, we got the message!" Nechama grinned. "Relax, Chani. We haven't been late yet — not even last month!"

Jen giggled. "Nechama...you're asking for it!"

"Who, me?" Nechama asked just a little too innocently.

The girls said their final goodbyes and "mazel tovs," walked out of the Farber home, and piled into the wagon. One by one Rabbi Orenstein dropped off the tired, happy girls at their homes.

Batya waved a cheery hand as she jumped out of the car. "We should go only to *simchos*, Batya," Mrs. Orenstein sang out.

Luckily a wandering cloud momentarily obscured the full moon, casting Batya's face in shadow. Otherwise, the glow on Batya's face might have given away her own secret.

Only for *simchos*. Batya shivered with delight as she thought about her own personal *simchah*, the secret her mother had told her not long before.

Would it be a boy? A girl? It didn't really matter. It would be the sister or brother she'd longed for for so many years. She wouldn't be the "only child" anymore.

Her mother was going to have a baby. Her baby.

For the Ben-Levi's, the *simchos* were just beginning.

The B.Y. Times

Nisan, Vol. II, No. 7

RAVE REVIEWS

It's already been a month since the fabulous Purim Festival, but the memories are still fresh in our minds. The entire day was a celebration of achdus, as all the girls worked together to make the Festival so special. Everyone had a marvelous time -- from the girls running the booths to their customers, from the mothers to their daughters to their teachers, from the girls who put on the Purimshpiel to the teachers who put on a Purimshpiel of their own, imitating the girls! (Rebbetzin Falovitz makes a great Nechama Orenstein!) Everyone worked together, laughed together, and had a great time together. There's no way the Festival could've been such a great success if everyone -- the Student Council members, the eighth grade class, and the whole Bais Yaakov student body -- hadn't all pitched in and lent a hand. It just goes to show: with achdus, anything -- and everything -- is possible!

THE CHOFETZ CHAIM SEZ

If somebody tells you a secret, you're not allowed to repeat it. Information is considered a secret if your friend tells only you and one other person. If she tells it to three or more people, you can assume she doesn't mind if it gets around. But if she specifies that you shouldn't tell anyone about it, you're not allowed to tell anyone, even if she told you in the presence of several others.

A secret doesn't have to be lashon hara to make it asur for you to pass it on. Any information your friend gives you has to be kept a secret if she doesn't want it spread around. If you tell a friend's secret to somebody else, you might embarrass her -- and that's not allowed, either!

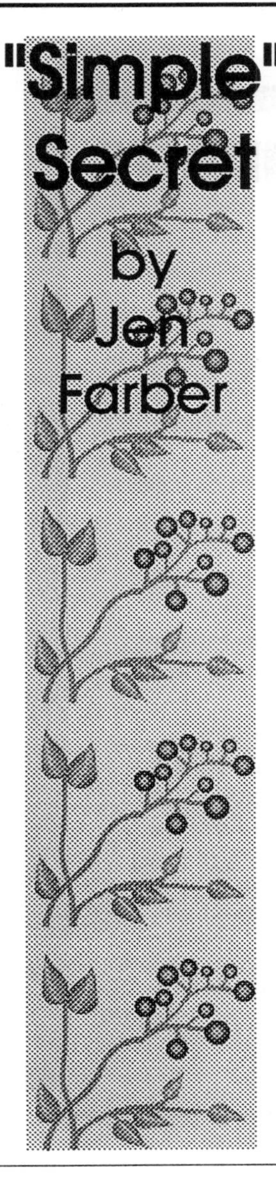

I told my friend a secret
I whispered in her ear
A juicy, nasty secret
That no one else could hear.
I knew it wasn't proper
I knew I shouldn't do it
But it would stay a secret
And that's all there was to it...

But someone else was watching
Another classmate knew
And she felt very curious --
She wanted to hear, too.
And so she asked my friend to tell
The secret that she'd heard
My friend agreed, but asked her
Not to ever say a word...

And so the secret travelled
With hurried, whispered talk
From one girl to another friend
The nasty secret stalked,
And finally it reached the ears
Of whom it was about
And then my juicy, nasty secret
Finally came out.

I told my friend a secret
I thought it did no harm
And she told just one other girl
She didn't feel alarmed.
I told my friend a secret
And I regret it in the end
Because I told that secret
I now have lost a friend.

Wow, it's been a real simchadik month! The B.Y. Times wishes a warm mazel tov to the following girls:

First grade: Michal Brenner, Aliza Katz, and Sarah Bodner, on the birth of a baby brother or sister.
Second grade: Kayla Goldberg on the bar mitzvah of her brother.
Third grade: Simi Feinberg on the birth of a baby sister. Shani Markstien on her sister's engagement.
Fourth grade: Melissa Farber on her brother's engagement. Mimi Bodner -- see above!
Fifth grade: Chayala Milstein, Brochie Nusbaum, Nechama Katz, and Devorah Feinberg, on the birth of a baby brother or sister.
Sixth grade: Tzivia Berkowitz on her sister's engagement and the birth of a baby brother!
Seventh grade: Jen Farber -- see above! Batya Ben Levi, on the birth of a "surrogate nephew."
Eighth grade: Faigie Munk on the birth of a baby sister. Tehilla Lieber on the engagement of her sister.

Mazel tov, and im yirtzeh Hashem by us all!!

President's Piece

by Chinky Chinn

The students of Bais Yaakov of Bloomfield have once again displayed a tremendous outpouring of chesed. We've gotten fabulous responses to our request for volunteers to help out mothers with heavy workloads right before Pesach. Washing dishes, folding laundry, keeping the kids occupied -- no matter what the chore, our volunteers did it all with a smile.

The Student Council has received dozens of phone calls from mothers, thanking Bais Yaakov for helping them when they needed it most. The Chesed Project is still going strong, so it's not too late to pitch in and join us if you haven't yet! It makes me proud to be a Bloomfielder -- to live in a city with such achdus, where everyone is ready to help another person in need. A chag kosher v'sameach to us all!

GO AROUND IN CIRCLES--AND ENJOY!

RINK-AROUND-THE-ROSIE,

Bloomfield's biggest rollerskating rink, offers new hours--and new discounts--just for B.Y. of Bloomfield girls.

Skate to the sounds of Avi Shoham and your other favorite singers, every Sunday from 3 p.m. to 7 p.m., and Tuesday nights from 6 p.m. to 8 p.m.

SEE YOU THERE!

The Recipe Corner

Pesach Strawberry Ice Cream (and all year, too!)

1 quart strawberries
3/4 c. sugar
two egg whites
juice of one lemon

1. Break open eggs and separate whites from yolks. (Check for blood spots!) Put egg whites in mixing bowl. (Cover the egg yolks and stick them in the fridge. You don't need them.)
2. Wash off strawberries and cut off green tops. Pour into bowl, saving a few strawberries to use as garnish.
3. Add sugar and lemon juice.
4. Whip on high speed for at least ten minutes, until it's high and pink and fluffy. Pour into container and freeze. Serve with half a strawberry on top. Yummy!

We've got the cheese!

BEN-LEVI'S PIZZA SHOP

Sunday Special:
FREE bottle of soda with every pie!
157 Oak Street (corner of Central Ave.)

Editorial

The Jews suffered in Mitzrayim for two hundred and ten long years. They were slaves, with barely anything to eat and no encouragement in sight. Nevertheless, they stubbornly remained Jews. There were three things they refused to change: the way they dressed, the language they spoke, and their names. These three things helped differentiate them from the Egyptians and kept them together as a nation.

Today, there are many things that differentiate us from the nations around us: Shabbos, the Yomim Tovim, and the way we dress (I mean tzenius, not the uniforms!), to name only a few. But all our differences have one thing in common: they keep us one nation, together. It's always been that way, from the time of the Churban Beis Hamikdash, when the Jews were the only nation who refused to accept Rome's idolatry, to the generations of European Jews who spoke Yiddish to keep themselves apart from the nations surrounding them.

"In every generation, our enemies have arisen to destroy us, and Hashem saves us from their hand." Destruction has threatened the Jewish nation again and again, but we have always refused to assimilate and remained true Jews. We, in our time, have witnessed such a miracle during the Gulf War. And now, with Pesach just around the corner, let us continue to work on our achdus. The second Beis Hamikdash was destroyed because of senseless hatred that drove Jews apart; with achdus, we can help to bring the geulah sheleimah, bimheirah viyameinu, amein!

The B.Y. Slimes

Ahh Choo!

by Chani Cough-man
Editor-in-Relief

It's that time of year again -- you know, Adar. When my allergies act up. I'm allergic to anything that requires any serious thought, planning, or work (ahh choo!). Particularly assigning articles, calling staff meetings, making sure everyone does their jobs. On top of all that, we've got tons of tests and homework (cough, cough). I need to renew my prescription for anti-testamines. I'm signing off now, folks. Pass the Kleenex!

Class Fib-bits

Congratulations to the sixth graders for getting Mrs. S. to postpone that math test!

Thank you, Ilana Silver, assistant distribution editor for donating two tons of potato chips to the Purimshpiel. Finally some sensible food.

Congratulations to the B.Y. Slimes staff for getting a new photocopy machine. Now you readers can catch all the typos.

Jen Farber's brother Jack, who broke out Color War

last year with his private plane, has agreed to give free plane rides every day during recess for the month of Adar. Up, up, and away!

Loshon Hara Column
Guaranteed to make your ears pop off!

King Achashverush invited Vashti to his party. When she said no way, he didn't believe her "tall tail."

What does Haman do during vacation? Just hangs around.

What was Noach's favorite cake? "Mabul" cake.

Recipes that will turn your stomach and rot your teeth

Kreplach and Caramel Sauce
by Sticky Chinn

1. Get your mom to do the hard stuff -- make the kreplach.
2. Melt some caramels over a double boiler
3. Serve kreplach with caramel goo-sauce.
4. Make appointment with your favorite dentist.

President Chinnton Presents Teachers with New Health Plan

by Zehava Sharvit

President Chinky Chinnton explained her new health plan to teachers last week. The president claims that this plan is the best way to safeguard the health of the student body.

The president told teachers: "If any student desires a test, she's got thirty days to decide whether she wants to take it. If the student doesn't summon the teacher during that time....forget it!"

Try our latest—
Pea Pizza

Ben-Lazy's Pizza
We've got the peas
(too lazy to grate the cheese!)

P.S. Bring your own can opener!)

Redhead Club
Forming
call
Nechama Orangestein

Stylish Haircuts
make your appointments with Jen Barber

No offense meant to the B.Y. Times staff

HAVE A HAPPY PURIM!!!

11
Gila's Secret

Batya sat on her front porch, enjoying the unusually warm and sunny weather as she waited for her mother to join her. She smiled happily as she thought of the shopping trip they were taking. Who would have thought that Mrs. Ben Levi would be buying maternity clothes? Once her mother "went public," Batya would be able to share her joy with her friends. She couldn't wait!

The roar of a large moving van turning into her quiet street broke her happy reverie. Why, it was stopping just down the block, at the Millers' old house.

A mini-van pulled up behind the large truck. A bearded man leaped out and began an avid conversation with one of the movers. Great! Her new neighbors looked like they were *frum* people.

Batya's grin grew wider as she saw a girl follow

her father out of the mini-van. She looked, oh, just about Batya's age. Batya hoped they would hit it off. How nice to have a friend right on her block!

The sound of a jangling telephone sent Batya scurrying into the house.

Five hours and six dresses later, Batya and her mother staggered back into the house. With a sigh of relief, Mrs. Ben-Levi flung down her load of clothes boxes and bags onto the sofa.

"Wow, I can't believe shopping can be so exhausting," she said, flinging herself onto the sofa too.

"But fun, Ima, right?"

"Sure," her mother smiled.

Batya walked over to the window and gazed out. There was no sign of the moving truck, but the mini-van was parked in front of the house at the corner.

"Oh, Ima, I think we have new neighbors," Batya said. She told her mother about the moving van and the girl that she'd seen that morning.

"I was wondering if I could go over there and say hi. Kind of make her feel at home."

Mrs. Ben-Levi smiled. How like her considerate daughter! "Sure, Batya. And take over some brownies from the freezer. Explain to them that I'm a bit tired, but I hope to welcome them personally tomorrow morning."

Batya knocked at the cheerful white door. She looked with satisfaction at the mezuzah that had been affixed: Her neighbors hadn't wasted time getting that mitzvah done!

The door opened. The girl whom Batya had seen that morning stood before her.

Suddenly, Batya felt shy. "I'm...I'm Batya Ben-Levi. I live down the block. Um...that is...welcome." Feeling foolish, Batya held out the pretty plate of brownies.

"I'm Gila Schell. Thanks."

For a moment there was silence. Then Gila flashed a bright smile. "We just moved in from Riverside. Hi, neighbor."

Somehow, Gila's smile was the ice-breaker they needed. For the next ten minutes the two girls chatted, exchanged stories and impressions, as they stood on the doorstep. Gila had come from Riverside, a small community not far from Bloomfield. She was going to begin school next week and was happy to find out she'd be in Batya's class.

The time flew. Batya was thrilled with her new neighbor. She was vivacious, energetic—and a lot of fun.

Suddenly a figure emerged from within. Gila introduced Batya to her mother, Mrs. Schell.

"Why don't you invite Batya in, Gila," Mrs. Schell said, after thanking Batya for the brownies. "I'm sure she won't mind the mess," she added, with an engaging grin that reminded Batya of Gila.

She glanced at her new friend. Gila's face had gotten serious, almost sad. The grin was gone. "Another time, Ima, maybe," she said quietly.

Batya looked at her, puzzled. Gila looked really upset about Batya coming in. What was going on here?

As she made her way down the block she thought about her new neighbor. Why had Gila been so upset at the idea of Batya coming in? What did she have in her new house that she didn't want Batya to see?

What was Gila's secret?

A great new girl—with a great big secret? Read all about it in the next issue of the *B.Y. Times*.